ROYAL BLOOD

ROYAL BLOOD

BY

BRUCE WOODS

Royal Blood by Bruce Woods
Copyright © 2018 Bruce Woods

ISBN-13: 978-1-946409-84-3(Paperback)
ISBN   :-978-1-946409-85-0(e-book)

BISAC Subject Headings:
FIC031020FICTION / Thrillers / Historical
FIC009100 FICTION / Fantasy / Action & Adventure
FIC009070 FICTION / Fantasy / Dark Fantasy

Editing: Chris Paige
The Book Cover Whisperer:
ProfessionalBookCoverDesign.com

Address all correspondence to:

Penmore Press LLC
920 N Javelina Pl
Tucson AZ 85748

DEDICATION

For Mary Sonnichsen

"What strange phenomena we find in a great city, all we need do is stroll about with our eyes open. Life swarms with innocent monsters."

Charles Baudelaire

"Eulogy is nice, but one does not learn anything from it.
Ellen Terry

This is a work of fiction, and the fictional characters herein are, you know, fictional, and not meant to represent anyone living, dead, or undead. If any of them remind you of yourself or someone you know, you have my congratulations or sympathy, depending upon the character involved. It is also a work of historical fiction, however, and much research has gone into accurately representing the times and places portrayed. That said, when an historical personage in this work interacts with a fictional one, the result is of course wholly a figment of my imagination, and not meant to imply how that real individual did, or would, react to vampires and other such inconveniences.

As noted, I've gone to some lengths to research the period in which this novel is set, and hope that it will for the most part pass historical muster (saving the Steampunk elements, which, although sometimes quite nifty, are also pure fancy). Dutiful historians will, however, note that in some instances the chronology of the book will intentionally depart from historical accuracy to serve the needs of the story, since the past didn't always occur in the correct order. Any unintentional errors are the fault of the author and not of the various editors who have done so much to give this story whatever charm it might have.

Bruce Woods

CHAPTER 1

An encounter with Mr. Holmes—My surprise that he knows me—Discussion of the evening's entertainment--A mysterious invitation—The distinctive scents of the streets of London—A late repast.

On the evening when my adventure began, I was fortunate enough to be seated behind the incomparable Mr. Holmes at an otherwise forgettable lecture. The presentation itself was some claptrap about bringing the benefits of Victorian technology to the benighted colonies, but I much enjoyed the opportunity to so closely observe the Great Man at his leisure, if such a mind as his can ever be truly said to be at rest.

At one point I saw the detective draw his fingertip over the back of his right ear, and then sniff at the digit as if savoring the fragrance of a fine cigar. I wondered if he was indulging his curiosity about this most personal scent with an eye toward some planned new science of criminal identification; or perhaps evaluating his own well being by figuratively taking the temperature of the aroma, to note any variance from normalcy. I am something of a student of the body's perfumes myself, and watched entranced, wondering what other enthusiasms we might share.

These were all idle fancies on my part, to be sure. But then, as we were filing out of the hall, not much enlightened by the proceedings upon the podium, he turned to me, his trademark deerstalker still tucked under one arm.

"Did you enjoy the evening's program, Miss Monot?" he said with a genial smile.

Holmes and I had never been introduced, and, though I know men find me comely, I would not be so vain as to think that I had warranted his special notice for any reason. Still, such knowledge of a stranger's identity is not to be unexpected when displayed by the world's foremost detective.

"You have the advantage of me, sir," I responded. "For, although everyone of course knows your name and face, I cannot remember enjoying the honor of an introduction."

"Forgive my boldness, Miss!" he exclaimed. "We have mutual friends, it seems, and I have let my woolgathering cloud my propriety and failed to say so by way of introduction. If it would not offend, might we simply presume acquaintance, since we appear to already know each other, if at a distance?"

"It would be my pleasure, Mr. Holmes, if you so wish." I punctuated the words with a pretty curtsey as we left the tobacco-fogged womb of the hall for the less fragrant clouds of the London evening streets. "And to address your initial query, no, I fear the lecture has left me unmoved. I dare say the enlightened world's colonial subjects, and I use the collective term because America is innocent of neither envying nor emulating the great national power that she broke away from, would soon reduce steam-engine boilers to pots in which to cook us, and beat cogs into spearheads to better demonstrate their displeasure with our paternal guidance."

Holmes laughed; it was a surprisingly rich guffaw to spring from such a rapier-thin form.

"You might be right at that, Miss Monot, but it wouldn't do to underestimate our disadvantaged brethren. The human mind is no less developed or more lacking in wondrous powers for being deprived of gaslights and airships."

"I bow to your superior knowledge, Mr. Holmes," I said. I quite agreed with him, of course, having had some little experience with America's red Indians, and knowing full well that they were no one's inferiors in terms of natural intellectual abilities.

"Not at all, not at all," the detective replied. "I relish the crossed blades of intelligent discourse." Here he slipped an embossed card from a brass and leather case plucked from his waistcoat pocket with long and agile fingers. "In fact, perhaps you'd be so kind as to join me and a pair of my acquaintances for a lively discussion of related issues at my Baker Street quarters tomorrow evening at eight? I promise it will be more entertaining than the lecture we've both just endured, and it will be a proper gathering, of course. You will not be the only member of the frail sex in attendance."

I took the card and thanked him; wondering if, though I'd arrived after the Detective, chance had truly led to my sitting behind him, or whether it was the result of some intricately choreographed plot that only a mind such as his could imagine and engineer.

The question remained with me as I mounted my Horace-Wilkershire Coilcycle, raised the kick stand and pulled free the lever that allows the huge inner mainspring to commence its mighty uncoiling. Silently, save for the occasional slop of London street unmentionables against the undersides of my mechanical steed's fenders, I rolled back to my lodgings at a sprightly 20 m.p.h., glad for the freedom of my British jumpsuit (which would never have been tolerated at home on the more parochial streets of the District of Columbia), as well as for my half cape and goggles in the damp evening air, and thinking longingly about the joys of a nightcap of warm blood.

CHAPTER 2

A hot snack, sadly enough, was not in the offing. I had determined to make every effort to be on my best behavior while in a foreign land (and had promised my utmost discretion to the Mistress of the City when I paid my respects to that worthy on arrival). So, although a plethora of potential victims—drugged on one substance or another, already inert or almost so—tempted me on my ride home, I had to take my supper cold from the bottled stock which the Mistress had provided me, and to be appropriately thankful for the Carre' Ammonia Refrigerator I'd had the foresight to install in my quarters.

Perhaps it was that chilled weight poured late upon my stomach (it is, of course, never appropriate to re-heat blood, it becomes more of a pudding than a beverage in the process, and loses to the fire the very life which feeds us, a vitality which refrigeration preserves for a short while) that caused my dreams, rare things for me in the best of times, to list toward the strange. Regardless, though I was appropriately weary when I finished speaking my notes into the brass bell of my miniature Tessier-Ashpool Recording Device at 6:00 a.m., I never truly settled into the deep emptiness of sleep, and arose late the following afternoon feeling vaguely ill at ease and melancholy.

I, however, denied myself the indulgence of such a soft affliction. Anticipating the evening ahead, I selected a knee length coat-dress in tan, with zippered sleeves and enough pockets, D-rings, and buckles to accommodate anything I might be expected to carry to or from the gathering. I wore bloomers beneath, of course, to allow me to straddle my Coilcycle with decency, and knee-length button-boots with practical gum soles.

Dressed, I found myself with some time to spare before the soirée' I'd assented to. The lingering sunlight posed no more threat to me than it would to the fairest Scandinavian, but I had no pressing business in the world beyond my rooms until the appointed time, so I breakfasted lightly, no more than a cup or so, mindful of my disturbed sleep of the day before. While so partaking, I listened to my last recorded transcript, erasing and speaking edits into the device as necessary (the notes thus transcribed throughout my adventure assuring the relative accuracy of this memoire, which I hope will prove instructional and entertaining to at least some of my kin).

With that accomplished, the hour was appropriate, and my windows showed a welcoming darkness. Checking my appearance one final time and finding myself pleased (contrary to the exotic myths, a mirror has no more difficulty revealing my faults and advantages than it would those of any primping harlot or debutante), I took the steam lift to the basement. There, my Coilcycle was fully wound, courtesy of the driveshaft I'd had fitted to the main boiler at considerable expense (and thanks to the permission of my landlord and, no doubt, to the generous access fee that he had demanded).

The trusty vehicle seemed no less eager than I to set out upon the night's adventures, and fairly leapt ahead when I released its mainspring.   I sped through the darkened streets, surrounded by the miasma of fair and foul odors that I had come to associate with London; blood and urine and feces, coal smoke and perfume, fruits and meats and breads.

It was a heady brew, changing with each block and neighborhood; and not for the first time I thought that, with a bit more familiarity, I could blindly find my way among the city's lanes and alleys, lead along by such olfactory clues alone.

In short order I pulled to a stop at the upper end of Baker Street, my Cycle's coil whining against the restriction I levered onto it, as if not ready to so soon cut its run short. Flicking the kick stand in place and gently setting the weight of the Horace-Wilkershire upon it, I ascended the seventeen steps to the flat at 221B, wondering if my arrival were tracked through a finger-split slatted blind by the Famous Detective's landlady, the redoubtable Mrs. Hudson, in her ground floor dwelling.

Holmes himself answered the door, casually clad in a dark smoking jacket, slacks, and slippers.

"Miss Monot, a pleasure," he said. "I'm grateful for your punctuality, the lack of which I count as one of the more perverse indulgences to which our age is prone. Please, allow me to introduce you to my other guests."

Hanging my goggles and short cape on the hat tree in the entryway, I followed my host into a study, dark but not gloomy and redolent of a particularly pungent tobacco smoke. Neither the dimness of the room nor the clouds of the latter, however, obscured my view of the two individuals seated within. I confess that I hesitated in momentary confusion.

One, a stout and mustachioed gentleman who radiated power as a hard-run engine gives off heat, appeared familiar, as if I had seen his image or caricature in one of the papers of the day. It was the other who gave me pause, however, for I had paid my respects to the gray-eyed beauty when first setting foot into this town in which she, among our kind, enjoyed first pride of place and absolute power.

Noting my confusion, the Mistress of the City rose and stepped forward to meet me, offering her perfumed embrace.

"We meet again, Paulette Monot. Greetings girl, I trust you are enjoying your sojourn in our poor little metropolis."

"Lady Alice Ellen," I managed to breathe, earning her soft laugh that had so stolen the hearts of theatre audiences for lo these many decades.

"It is Ellen Terry, or Ellen alone, among this company, my sweet. Allow me to present my dear friend, and sponsor of the enterprise to which we invite you, the famous, though some would say infamous, Mr. Cecil Rhodes of South Africa."

The gentleman in question labored to his feet, and kissed my hand, that brief touch of lip upon skin revealing him as a man of great appetite, though not perhaps for female flesh. I murmured my greeting in turn, still unsure of my footing on these dangerous sands, and Miss Terry continued, the Celebrated Actress seeming almost gleeful at my apparent confusion.

"Please, comfort yourself, Paulette," she said. "There are no secrets among this trio, at least none of the sort that seems to concern you. Mr. Holmes has long been privy to the existence of our kind in London, and has exchanged favor for favor with us numerous times in the pursuit of his investigations. It is, in fact, in return for one such recent tit for tat that I have allowed him to ask your assistance tonight on behalf of Mr. Rhodes. It so happens that my darling Cecil (and here the large man harrumphed, if such a high-pitched exclamation can rightly be called by that name, before regaining his seat) is both a trusted friend of the kin and a sometimes business partner of mine. They know what we are, dear, so you can dispense of the mask you've so bravely and respectfully donned during your days in my city."

Digesting this information was as difficult as had been assimilating my cold repast of the night before, but I allowed Holmes to seat me in a leather armchair.

"You are among friends here, you see, Miss Monot," he said, "and I trust will have no need of the cunningly delicate pepper-box pistol so carefully concealed in your lower right coat pocket."

I began to stutter an apology, as much for the arrogance that had let me believe I could confound the Great Detective as for the faux pas of bringing a weapon into presumably friendly company, but he laughed off my attempt.

"Though you certainly require no such protection if you are half as formidable a creature as is the fascinating Miss Terry here, I applaud your foresight. London is a dangerous place for the most stalwart among us. I suspect there are both silver and hardwood slugs among the cartridges you've chambered, are there not?"

Here I allowed myself to blush fully as I nodded my confession, the feeling rare and hot along the high country of my cheekbones, which amused my companions greatly and seemed to, once their laughter had subsided, cue the beginning of the evening's discussions in earnest.

"Tell us, Miss Monot," began Holmes, "what do you know of the Dark Continent?"

"No more or less than one might expect of an Educated Person of this age," I admitted. "I am fortunate enough to have matriculated at Wells College, and thus benefitted from enlightenment as thorough as any available to American womanhood, and I am fairly diligent in keeping abreast of the news of the day."

"Capital," said the Detective, "for it is toward Africa that we turn our eyes here. It has recently come to our attention that Lobengula, Chief of the Matabele, has sent a raiding party against a number of villages in the Victoria district that were under the protection of the British South Africa Company. His army destroyed the native compounds, either killing or abducting all they found therein. When ordered by BSA officials to withdraw, Lobengula's Impi refused, and the two forces came to blows. The Matabele showed their heels after a taste of British firepower, but Rhodes and I believe that this can only be the start of a larger struggle; and, though the Company's police have the benefit of Maxim, Gardner, and Hotchkiss guns, their ranks of fighting men, even if swelled by loyal MaShona tribesmen, would be dwarfed by the armies the African King can call into play."

"This is not a matter of honor alone, Miss," Rhodes interjected, his high-pitched voice raised in seeming excitement. "The future of the Empire in Africa hangs in the balance, with the wealth of that immense nation as prize for the victor. Matabele-land must be England's!"

"Quite so," agreed Holmes, "And it is only the supreme importance of this issue that has led my colleague and I to approach Miss Terry to see if she might be able to offer aid."

I confess I was quite confounded at this point, both at the amount of information imparted and with curiosity at what role I might be expected to play. Thankfully, the Mistress of the City was quick to begin unraveling those knots.

"Have you ever heard rumor of the presence of our kind in Africa, Paulette?" she asked.

"I have not." I admitted. "I have been led to believe that our few are distributed among the Great Cities of Europe and

America, though many believe that kin could be present in Asia, and may be among the many mysteries that continent has yet to reveal."

"That has been the assumption held by most of us, certainly," Ellen replied, "but I for one have always wondered why Africa would be unblessed by our presence. And recent discoveries have further piqued my curiosity." Here she extended an elegant hand to Mr. Rhodes, who passed her a slim volume opened to a dog-eared page. The journal, for such it proved to be, was *The Empire Review*. The account to which she drew my attention, marked with thick pencil strokes, concerned an encounter a group of vacationers had while on their journey:

"He had approached the wagon in a somewhat begging pose," it read. *"There was a half-suppressed glitter in his eye, the corners of the sly, tight-lipped, cruel mouth were half lowered deprecatingly, and the vampire-like lines of his sharp cut features were besmoothed and straightened. But our host, Mr. Rhodes's representative, refused him food, and a sharp altercation took place between them. This suffered to alter the man's whole demeanor and demonstrate the latent viciousness, the elemental hate that possessed him. His yellow sunken eyes swelled forth— bloodshot—emitting an evil glare, the features became ragged and puckered with passion, the figure was bent and cowering as if for a spring, while his voice—by turns raucous and sibilant—poured imprecations on ourselves and our ancestors."*

I looked up from the volume, still nothing like convinced.

"But surely this is only the product of an excitable imagination and race hatred," I said. "The image is more nearly that of our kind found in the most lurid fiction than reflective of our reality, and it seems the poor creature asked for food, an unlikely request from one of our sort."

"Perceptive comments, indeed," answered Holmes, "though it might be that Cecil's man only assumed the creature was seeking food and not testing the waters for a feed of a different kind. The fact remains that after the vacationers had completed their holiday and took airship back to London, the British South Africa representative in question was found murdered." Here the detective caught my eyes and smiled. "His throat was torn out as if by an animal, Miss Monot, and other than a cup or so that stained the dust beneath his corpse, he was drained dry of blood."

My eyes were surely wide as Ellen Terry continued the discussion.

"This and other evidence leads us to believe that it is in fact possible that the kin, though perhaps in a benighted state, do exist in the area about to be thrown into war. If one of our kind were able to contact them and attach their energies to the cause of the Company, such an alliance might well be enough to turn the tide of battle. It would be an opportunity for a neonate such as yourself to secure fortune aplenty to settle herself for some centuries, Paulette Monot. And you have embarked on your recent travels in search of adventure, have you not?"

Excitement and fear are surely twins, and I could not determine which held the upper hand in my emotions at that moment.

"Tell me what you want me to do." I said.

CHAPTER 3

*The plan is hatched—Preparations for travel—Shopping
for safari—An evening with the Mistress of the City—
I encounter the* Boadicea

The plan was of necessity a vague one: I would travel
hence to Matabele-land under the pretence of tourism, and
attempt to make contact with my African kin, should they
indeed exist, by either locating them or making myself
possible to find. Though the warm blooded are not able to
spot us with any certainty, unless of course our feeding teeth
are unsheathed, we usually have no difficulty identifying one
another. (For one thing, an unchanged man or woman moves
to our eyes as if through a series of poses, with a brief stop at
each, rather like a projected film shot with too few frames
per minute, while the kin are in constant sweep and stride.
The difference is as clear to our eyes as that between a trudge
and a dance.)

Once contact was made (if all this wasn't, in fact, just a
wild fantasy that resulted in no more than an exotic sojourn
for yours truly), I would have access to various items with
which to buy my newfound kin's loyalty, and would, as far as
possible, play upon their sense of like cleaving to like.

With my agreement to undertake the adventure obtained,
preparations proceeded apace. I would begin the journey by
travelling to Vryburg, the striking off point for British
MaShona-land and Matabele-land, via modern means of

transportation, and set out from there with porters and wagons. I proposed to bring my Coilcycle, as well, and use it to range ahead of and to the side of my safari (for such are African journeys commonly called), the better to cover the ground. My sponsors assented to this, though Rhodes thought the vehicle's utility and indeed survival were unlikely under the Dark Continent's harsh conditions. In an attempt to answer such doubts, I had the wheels fitted with tires as heavily lugged as a walking-boot's sole, had a sturdier spring installed in its Earles leading-link front fork, and purchased an oversized double-ended lever for winding its spring. (The salesman warned me that the latter would perhaps prove far too much for a woman to handle; I only simpered and assured him that I would have ample help available.)

Thus the purely logistical details fell into place, predicted by the meticulous mind of Holmes, organized with the consummate professionalism of Miss Terry, and thoroughly lubricated with Rhodes' money. I myself purchased a few niceties to smooth the experience. Among these was a collapsible solar teapot of Irish manufacture, heated by a folding convex mirror and allowing the brewing of the beverage without access to fire (or tell-tale smoke). I of course had little appetite for tea, but I believed I would find it useful to pretend to savor it in order to keep up appearances. To the same end, I procured a clever portable water filter.

I looked without success for a cooling device small enough to transport by ox-wagon, but some things seemed still beyond even the overarching reach of the scientists of our day. I resigned myself to a combination of abstinence and cautious human predation while travelling, and reluctantly accepted that I was likely to be limited to dietary bestiality (for although animal blood may nourish, it never pleases) when I finally arrived in the wilds of Matabele-land.

With the last in mind, another purchase that I found myself quite pleased with was that of a Gibbs-Farquaharson-Metford rifle taking a 360 No. 3 Express cartridge. The falling block action of the little gun was quite elegant, and, upon trying it out at Rhodes' private range, I found its Metford-rifled barrel produced great and consistent accuracy. It was, of course, only a single-shot, but if my aim were true with the first bullet I hoped there would be less need for the second. Should there ever be, I would have access to my pepper-pot pistol (though this was of little use at any great range).

If I were to appear to be on safari, after all, it stood to reason that I would have to be prepared to shoot something; and I reckoned the Gibbs, with soft or solid bullets as the situation required, would be adequate for anything less than an elephant, which I had little desire to fire at in any case. The smaller antelopes I would, I assumed, be able to run down without aid of a firearm, though I knew it would be incautious to do so within sight of my bearers.

Soon after these and a scattering of other purchases were obtained and mastered, it was time for my departure. Before I set forth, however, I was treated to an evening in the company of the Mistress of the City. She began by explaining my rather complex itinerary. Cognizant of my needs, she had arranged for alternate legs of the journey on airship, steamer, and train, allowing me the most efficient forms of travel as well as time to roam (and hunt for human prey) in population centers along the way. She would accompany me on the first leg, a relatively brief ride in a luxury dirigible to Paris, where she had business with her French counterpart.

I was of course grateful for the care she had put into planning my lengthy travels, and for her company on the initial jaunt, but more so for the repast she offered me that evening. She had arranged for a lovely pair of young adults, brother and sister they certainly were, likely children of some country squire, to be delivered to us under enchantment, and even did me the honor of allowing me to perform the small dip of scalpel into wrist which opened her choice for her. We sipped leisurely, and talked, and it was a most pleasant and enlightening experience. Though drugged or bedazzled blood is always to my mind to be considered third to that given willingly and that taken by chase, the charming nature of my companion's company elevated the dining experience to among the most enjoyable I've ever experienced.

The youngsters were removed after feeding to wake from a long sleep little the worse for wear; though the lost hours they shared that night might become a cherished mystery, jointly held, that could keep them close as the passage of years tries to pry them apart.

Even the most magical of encounters must end, however, and not long thereafter Ellen Terry and I were boarding the airship *Boadicea* for the first leg of my journey. The process of entering the great craft was akin to stepping up a ladder onto the deck of a boat at dock. The huge vehicle, though tied down, was never perfectly still, shuddering and straining against the restraints that held her from the heights to which she aspired.

CHAPTER 4

An aerial experience—Compact quarters—Ingenious appointments—The pleasure of Her company—Going Native in Egypt—The mysterious marketplace—The game's afoot!—A pretty hunt, indeed—A dinner worth waiting for.

I was thrilled to finally have the opportunity to travel by airship, having made the journey from America to London by boat. (That passage itself had been difficult for someone as young to the kin as I was. Fortunately, I had soon learned that, though I had not yet mastered the trick of capturing my intended with a glance as older individuals of my kind can, there were adequate numbers of gentlemen aboard my ship who were quite willing to stare into a young woman's eyes long enough for even my still poorly-tempered will to entrance them.)

I found the quarters on the *Boadicea*, albeit undoubtedly elegant, to be even more cramped than those I'd enjoyed at sea. Though the airship's great, ovoid-ribbed envelope measured almost 8,000 feet from end to end, she was only equipped to carry 20 passengers. Miss Terry and I had adjoining rooms along one of the outer bulkheads. These were small but exquisitely well thought out. Though barely seven feet long and six wide, each room included a convertible bed, a chair, and a desk that folded flat against the wall when not in use. There was a pair of windows, as well, capable of being cracked, but not fully opened, by means of sturdy levers affixed to their rims.

Because our lodgings were against the outer wall, we each also had access to a small multi-purpose driveshaft. These were powered by tiny windmills that could be exposed to the rush of air against the cabin's external surface by means of hand cranks within the room. By manipulating a selection of pulleys, belts, and a clever system of gears, they could be used to power fans to cool the air, rotate the various cylinders on the in-room music box, or even coax thin, yellow illumination from the Edison-Swan electric bulbs set in the center of the ceilings.

All in all, I quite enjoyed my first experience of flight, and whilst savoring it became convinced that the ability to see large segments of land from far above, and to observe the chessboard of field and hedge, farm and village, would soon revolutionize mapmaking and change the way we think of distance. I was able to spend much of the trip in the company of Miss Terry, as well, and to properly thank her for the opportunity she had presented me in setting me this task. It was a gift of potentially incalculable value, and she had offered it to me in spite (or perhaps because) of the fact I was a mere naive child among the kin and a guest in her land.

Within no more than four hours, though, the *Boadicea* had landed in Paris, and the rest of my journey began. I'm afraid that this, by far the longer portion of my trip, was chiefly memorable for being tedious and, since I was forced to constantly either suffer hunger or search for opportunities to feed, frankly difficult to enjoy. This is not, of course, to say that there were not moments of interest along the way. I'll describe one such event here by way of example.

Having arrived in Cairo and with a day to explore before my next rail connection was due to depart, I established myself at a tolerable hotel (the d'Angleterre, as even at that time the more luxurious Shepheard's was quite overrun with tourists and insulated from the old city) and, after donning a dark *jilaabah* I'd arranged for the concierge to acquire for me, set out into the early evening streets.

The above-mentioned garment was made of a finely-woven black cotton and, with my blue eyes covered by a veil, allowed me to move with some anonymity among the crowd of late shoppers and early diners.

Before I left the city, I was to discover and become enamored of the then fashionable blue-tinted glasses to relieve the effects of the sun. I arranged for a pair to correct a slight impediment in my vision, which vanity had forbid me to deal with previously, and have worn such ever since.

As I wandered, I at first limited myself to exploring in order to learn the lay of the land in the area close to my hotel (as I did not want to stray so recklessly that I might have difficulty finding my way back). The rich and complex aromas of the marketplace were initially overwhelming, even to a girl familiar with the rank perfumes of the London streets, but before too long my senses acclimated themselves; as a loud clock's ticking will seem impossible to ignore upon first entering a room, only to fade from notice in a very short while.

I hadn't wandered far before I noticed the activity of a pickpocket working the crowd. I use the term loosely, as he was rather a thief of opportunity; slipping an item from the stall of an unwary shopkeeper here and deftly snipping a length of gold or silver chain from a strolling shopper there; pedestrians with actual pockets not being as numerous as they would be on a American or British lane.

Some of the kin rather pompously (I think) attest that they only prey upon the criminal element, but I have not been so constantly judicial in my hunting. That is not to say, however, that I don't relish the chance to see myself as society's avenging angel when that option presents itself. If in this case the "criminal" was more an impoverished entrepreneur than a monster, I can only say that opportunity quibbled about is opportunity lost.

I followed my intended prey for a time, admiring both his skill and his audaciousness. He was quite young, I saw, perhaps not even out of his teenage years, and his victims, though not the super-rich to whose control the pulleys and gears of the great world responded, were certainly far better off than he and, I think, suffered more anger than painful loss as a result of his depredations. At another time I might have let myself be dissuaded by such musings, but I had been dancing with hunger and boredom for too long, and once I had marked him was unable to convince myself to seek more worthy (that is to say, *unworthy*) prey.

It wasn't terribly long before he became aware that he was under surveillance, though I don't think that he initially suspected me. He was a creature used to detection and pursuit, I imagine, and thus the related instincts would have been more highly developed in him than in the masses. At any rate he increased his pace and began to weave a tortuous passage through the market, ducking down alleyways barely as wide as the span of his shoulders and dodging between and behind stalls.

I had no trouble following, and was even able to do so without, I think, drawing undue attention to myself. Eventually he resorted to full flight down a long and empty alleyway. Of course I was upon him in an instant, though in my brief run I had time to admire the way my *jilaabah* flared in the speed of the chase. I confess I felt a small pleasure at this spectacle's unintended nod to the hoary bat-legends of Europe, and wondered if I might yet, perhaps unwittingly, spark another such tale here in myth-ridden Egypt.

He tried to scream as I bore him down, too panicked, I reckon, to wonder at my being a woman or to hope my desires were more natural, but he had not the breath for any volume. I clubbed him unconscious with the heel of my hand nonetheless, and stretched out his neck. He smelt of fear and unwashed skin and some pungent oil apparently meant to disguise the latter. He tasted young and delicious and stronger than I would have expected; apparently petty thieving and occasional flight had at least kept him well fed and fit. I left him with enough blood to wake weakly and to wonder; then straightened my all-concealing clothing and, head slightly bowed in a manner appropriate to my gender in this city, returned considerably happier and more comfortable to my hotel.

CHAPTER 5

Arrival in Vryburg—An illustrious escort appears—Eyes to rival those of the kin--The Legendary Hunter—My firearm meets his approval—A last rest within four walls.

Such entertainments were all too rare during my long passage to Vryburg, most of which would, I fear, make for a wearying read. Suffice to say I did arrive, with a small mountain of luggage; and found myself on the railroad platform, sleeved and gloved and broad-hatted against the equatorial sun. I was confident that my employers would not leave me to my own devices in such a foreign place and, sure enough, I had barely begun to inventory my steamer trunks and other baggage before I was approached by a gentleman who identified himself as being in the service of Mr. Rhodes.

He was a striking individual. Though of average height, he had that rare presence which transcends mere stature. He was bearded and mustachioed, though not in the rampant and bushy style common in the African colonies; instead, he was neatly groomed and the shape of his gracefully pointed beard seemed to perfectly compliment his thin, fine-featured face. He wore a grey double-Terai slouch hat, knickers, and a shirt open at the neck with a handkerchief knotted beneath.

His most remarkable features, however, were his eyes; bright blue and clear, and so powerful in influence that I for a moment wondered whether he might be kin. This thought was quickly dispelled, however; though graceful, he moved like a mortal. Still, and for all the fact that although I am a neonate I am not unschooled in the ways of the world, I found myself tempted to allow a blush under the weight of his polite attention.

"Miss Monot, I presume?" He said, a twinkle in those eyes marking his allusion to Mr. Stanley's famed exclamation on meeting with Dr. Livingston. "My name is Frederick Courtney Selous. Our mutual friend Mr. Cecil Rhodes arranged for me to meet you and to assist in preparations for our trip into Matabele-land. I trust your travels have not wearied you overmuch, for I fear you still have some ways to go."

"Mr. Selous," I replied, giving him my hand, "any concerns I might have had about the way ahead have melted with the knowledge that you will be lending me your assistance." I was of course familiar with the reputation of the Great Hunter, having used the dreary days of my journey to better familiarize myself with the recent history of the area to which I would be travelling. Indeed, the compliment I paid to him was no shallow courtliness; probably no European alive knew better the trails and dangers of the interior of Southern Africa; here was a man who had successfully sparred with Lobengula's own witch doctors, and in so doing won the grudging admiration of the infamous and mercurial-tempered Native King.

Selous had an ox-cart at the ready to carry my belongings to the rooms he had arranged, where I would be allowed to refresh myself before beginning the long trek ahead. While overseeing the loading of this (and noting my Coilcycle with no more than the politest of raised eyebrows) he spotted my hard-leather rifle case and glanced up at me, a hand on its grip.

"Would you mind if I had a look, Miss Monot? I've a rather keen interest in firearms."

I of course assented; and not a little smugly, I admit, for my reading had told me of his own preference for the products of Mr. Gibbs of Bristol. In this I was not disappointed, for his face lit up with an almost boyish smile as he removed the rifle from its case.

"A beautiful piece, and by one of the most accomplished of London's gunsmiths!" he remarked, checking the action and lifting the barrel to peer at the sky through it in order to better view the rifling within. "Some would consider it a light caliber for Africa, to be sure, but I've become something of an advocate for such, and am certain your selection will be more than adequate for most game. I will, of course, make sure that your gun bearer is equipped with something larger, should your camp be troubled by elephants, rhinoceros, or buffalo. Keep your Gibbs clean, Miss Monot, and do not rely upon your camp staff to make sure that insects have not nested in the barrel overnight, and it will serve you wonderfully well."

I was, of course, quite gratified by this endorsement of my choice, and assured the Hunter that I would take his advice to heart. With the ox-cart loaded to groaning, Mr. Selous introduced me to the bay horse he had acquired for me. (She would be a better shooting platform when in the pursuit of game than my Cycle, he assured me, and was "salted," and thus immune to the effects of the bite of the tsetse fly, which are generally fatal to horse and ox.) He then escorted me to my lodging, and the last rest I would enjoy within four solid walls for quite some time.

CHAPTER 6

I meet my safari crew—Selous gives them marching orders—Shooting for the pot—Melissa proves unworthy—My first kill—Unexpected company—An interrogation—Solving a personnel problem—The symbolism of vultures.

The staff that Mr. Selous had assembled for me included a cook (Joseph), a gun-bearer (Michael), a guide/major domo from the MaShona tribe (Thomas), 20 porters, 3 pack horses, my shooting bay (which I named Melissa), and a two-ox wagon; the animals charged with pulling the latter were also proofed against the dread disease. After stiffening the safari's resolve with some rather fierce admonitions, the Great Hunter went his own way on another errand for Mr. Rhodes, promising to cross paths with me before I actually entered the realm of the Matabele.

Encouraged as they were by Mr. Selous' stout words, my crew showed little dismay at my demand that we begin our marches in early morning, quite before full sunrise, break in the heat of the day, and trek again late into the evening. We were two days into the march when we began to see game, and the boys (for such they were called, youth or man or elder, back in the day) begged me to shoot something, as they were weary of their diet of mealy-meal. (This, a sort of crude corn mush, is the fuel upon which most of Africa runs, but meat is the preferred food when on a trek.) With an aim to satisfy their cravings (and my own), I slipped my Gibbs into a saddle scabbard, mounted Melissa, and set off in search of something for the pot.

Not a mile from camp I spotted a small herd of wildebeests, the ungainly creatures looking like the misbegotten offspring of antelope and buffalo. Riding parallel to their course of direction and gradually converging with the creatures, I was soon within rifle range and, slipping my weapon free from its wrap, pulled Melissa to a stop.

Success was not to be mine, however; for despite her reputation, the pony began to wander forward whenever I attempted to draw a bead, seemingly assuming that the next patch of yellow-dry grass was sweeter than that beneath her nose, and thus quite ruining my aim. This happened on three separate occasions before I turned her back toward camp in disgust. The disappointment on the faces of the porters was palpable as I rode in empty handed, so I decided to venture out again on the Coilcycle, in which I actually had far greater faith.

The Earles fork and knobbed tires with which I had fitted the mechanical steed had already proven quite equal to handing the trails we travelled, which were for the most part well packed by the passage of man and beast. The silence of its mainspring power allowed me to move into a position ahead of the slowly wandering herd and, putting the side stand down, I placed my hat atop the handlebars to cushion the Gibbs and found that this made for an admirable rest.

I took the first wildebeest on the point of the shoulder and he dropped in his tracks. Reloading quickly, I was able to give a second a quartering away shot that, I later discovered, took out the top of its heart. The animal ran some 50 yards before dropping, though I think it was dead on its feet for some part of that. I knew my people would come rushing forward at the sound of the shooting, so took only a moment to sip from the nearest, rapidly dying beast before chambering another round (an empty gun is less than worthless in the bush, as it might offer comfort and lead to complacency, while being little more useful than an awkward club if so called upon) and awaiting their arrival.

They weren't long in coming, though I had cautioned them to wait well back so as not to interfere with my chance at a shot (and to allow me a moment of privacy for my poor luncheon). Indeed, I believe it is only due to the respect they had for Mr. Selous (and the ferocity of his instructions to them) that they obeyed me as well as they did. Certainly it was the first time any of my group had trekked in a party led by a single woman, but such was his authority that I was never to encounter outright insubordination, and this sort of over-eagerness was the worst disobedience with which I would have to contend.

The wildebeest were butchered out in amazingly short order, and several small cook fires sprung up just beyond the carcasses, at which the fairest and fattest tit-bits were soon being roasted on sticks and happily consumed while no better than half raw and half charred. Into the middle of this wild scene wandered a lone individual from a nearby village, begging for a bit of meat. I called upon Thomas to translate and informed him that he was free to join the boys at one of the fires if he would provide me with information.

This he agreed to with enthusiasm, and soon shared the knowledge that Lobengula was keeping his Impis on the move, recruiting (or more likely conscripting) additional warriors from whatever villages he passed. The Dreaded King, it seems, was hesitant to confront the forces of the Company despite his long odds, and was struggling to control the younger of his warriors, who had never had the opportunity to wet their assegais in British blood and so believed it would be child's play to wipe the white men from their land. Hotter heads were likely to prevail, my informant opined, and the resulting conflagration would likely first spark along the Shangani River.

My informant was less forthcoming when I inquired, circumspectly you can be sure, about the presence of other individuals in the area, particularly those that preferred to be about by night, and hunted not the beasts of the veldt but human prey. His nervousness at this line of questioning told me much, and proved to be the only information on the subject I could draw out of him. So I eventually thanked him and bade him join the group at the nearest fire, where I think he counted himself lucky to be allowed to partake of only the leanest (and thus least desirable) of the offerings.

By the time we had returned to camp, my Cycle's mainspring was in need of tightening, and I determined to take advantage of this opportunity to solve a small staff problem that had come to my attention. One of the porters, who rejoiced in the name of Robert, a huge and powerful individual, had come to think of himself as a guard and not a bearer, and diligently patrolled the surroundings with his spear but was unwilling to carry a load. Thomas had proved unwilling or unable to bring this man to heel, perhaps fearful of the results of such a confrontation, so I had the brute brought to me.

Aided by my major domo's translation, I explained the winding of the Coilcycle's power source, displaying the great two-handed iron lever used for this task and implying that only the strongest of men could do such a job to my satisfaction. This played to his ego as I had hoped, and he gladly accepted responsibility for the daily chore. To my pleasure, he was to quickly learn to do other bits of routine maintenance, such as oiling the chain, removing thorns from the tires each night, and even changing and patching inner tubes when required. I believe he would have made a very capable mechanic had he been given the appropriate tools and time enough to learn the intricacies of the other tasks involved.

With the camp set to rights, I took tea and a small dinner into my tent (as it was my practice to pretend to eat in private, thus avoiding the most obvious questions about my nature), and recorded my thoughts upon the day into my Tessier-Ashpool. I had been particularly stricken by how rapidly the vultures had descended upon the carcasses. Appearing first as only the faintest black spots against the sky, the grim creatures drifted down on steep spirals, and in moments covered the remains of the two wildebeest, looking not like birds but like huge, dark maggots twining and swarming one atop the other as they struggled to feed upon the offal and what few scraps my own careful and greedy butchers had missed.

This spectacle led me to muse upon how events, once set in motion, can accelerate at a terrible pace, and be upon one, carrying unforeseen consequences, with an unanticipated velocity.

CHAPTER 7

The Matabele attack!—I escape my tent—Close combat in darkness—I order my men to flee—Revenge is sweet—A ride into the night—Asleep in a hollow tree —A joyous reunion—Chasing down an impala—An apparition appears—A deal is struck—His name is Shaka—I meet up with Selous again.

We trekked for some hours after dinner, as was our pattern, and made camp in full darkness in a pretty piece of veldt close by a waterhole that was not too sullied by animal activity. I was in my tent recording the day's notes into my device when I heard Robert's bellow of challenge from the edge of camp. This was followed close at hand with a scream of pain in another voice, which told me immediately that he had encountered interlopers and that my erstwhile Mechanic had wet his spear in the blood of at least one of the enemy. Immediately thereafter the night's quiet was further broken by the distinctive hollow booming of black powder guns, and I knew we were under attack in earnest.

Moving rapidly, I threw on my many-pocketed coat, grabbed and shouldered the heavy cartridge bag that was always close to my cot and, Gibbs in hand, flew out of the tent into a scene of rapidly developing chaos. The Matabele, for it was immediately clear that our assailants were of that tribe, were laying about them with assegai and nine-pound Martini-Henry rifles. A few members of my staff was putting up a spirited defense; Michael and Thomas using the 500 Nitro Express double rifles which Selous had provided them to defend the safari against large animals, and Robert, still standing, was a whirling dervish with his spear. Of Joseph the cook and the rest of the porters nothing was to be seen, and I feared them all either dead or fled.

I emptied my pepper-box into the closest of the enemies and then, taking cover behind my Coilcycle, took advantage of the superior night vision of my kind to pick off the Matabele riflemen with my Gibbs. Though I was quite proficient at rapidly reloading the weapon, it was still limited in firepower by virtue of the fact that the Farquaharson is a single-shot action; and though I determined that the attackers were not a full Impi but a raiding party of perhaps some three dozen warriors, it soon became clear that our stand, however hard fought, was doomed to fail. My rifle had grown hot with firing, and I feared a cartridge jam might result, so when Thomas, Michael, and Robert followed the sound of my shots to my side, I ordered them to flee along the route we had been traveling while I provided covering fire. I hoped that we could meet up with Selous' safari as planned by taking this course of flight, and I feared that, should my people retreat willy-nilly, my chances of finding them again would be slim.

Only two warriors from the raiding party tried to pursue my retreating men, the rest already busying themselves with evaluating, and in some cases fighting over, the spoils of our camp. I was able to drop the pair with two rounds from the Gibbs. Then, before those shots could attract additional unwelcome attention, I mounted the Coilcycle, with its headlamp off and with gratitude for its almost silent running, and rolled away down the path that Robert, Michael, and Thomas had taken.

Once I was well clear of our tents, and certain that I hadn't dragged my own pursuers along, I locked down the mainspring, left my vehicle and, moving quietly, taking full advantage of my night vision and what cover there was, crept back to the perimeter of the camp.

It was a scene worthy of Dante's Great Epic. The pillagers had built up our campfires, the better to see the treasures we had left behind, and the leaping flames and wildly costumed bodies made for a fascinating, if horrible, spectacle. I slipped carefully around the perimeter of the site until I was able to identify a single Matabele squatting on his heels some distance from his compatriots, apparently to enjoy a feast of pilfered wildebeest without fear of interruption or confiscation.

I took him from behind. There was more than strength enough in my small hands to shut off his throat and end any risk of raised alarm, and I dragged him further into the shadows before I fed to repletion, during which his eyes went from wild and wide with superstitious panic to an empty dullness. He was a sizable man, and I cannot say for certain whether I left him dead or no, but when I remounted my Cycle and whispered off into the darkness my mood was very much improved.

Once I'd put the camp perhaps a mile behind me, I paused to light the handlebar-mounted gas lamp. The illumination thus provided was quite unnecessary for my purposes, but I hoped it would give large game advance notice of my approach, and thus reduce the likelihood of a surprise confrontation.

In that manner I rode for some time, undisturbed save for the occasional startled crashing of some alarmed beast in the dark bush to either side of the sometimes narrow trail. I thought pursuit unlikely, as we had inflicted considerable damage in our losing defense, and I believed the surviving attackers had more of an appetite for plunder than they did for renewed hostilities. Still, the Coilcycle's track was quite unlike anything old Africa had ever seen, and would be easy to follow until wind or rain cleansed it away.

The ride was quite peaceful, truth be told. I was confident that I'd be able to make contact with my trio of helpmates before too long, and the night air was cool, soft, and fragrant. Certainly I gave some moments to mourn those who had been killed or wounded in the altercation, but consoled myself with the belief that the lion's share of my camp (perhaps not the best metaphor to use under the circumstances) had made good their escape and lost little more than the security of wages that the safari would have provided.

It might seem strange to the reader, but I had little fear for myself. I believed that I was quite equal to the challenges that might be posed by beast or country or hostile tribesmen. I had my pepper-box and Gibbs, after all, and ammunition enough for each in my cartridge bag; and of course I had my own strength and speed, all in all more imposing weapons and not subject to the need to reload. In short, if the Dark Continent wanted to test Paulette Monot, I felt quite ready for the questioning to begin.

After I'd ridden a good ten miles, I began looking for shelter, knowing that the tropical sunrise provided a far briefer transition between night and day than we of northern latitudes are accustomed to. I soon located a baobab tree, the trunk of which had been hollowed out enough by age and parasites for me to curl within. Once I'd used a stick to sweep it out (and assure myself that the cavity was not the nocturnal home of any dangerous snakes), I hid my machine in some nearby brush and made what bed I could within it.

I awoke with sunset approaching, immediately aware of stealthy movement in the bush not 200 yards away. I uncoiled quietly, brushing away the insects that had found their way onto my sleeping self, and, braced for action, letting my senses sweep the area. I quickly determined that it was not a Matabele hunting party but Robert, Michael, and Thomas, whom I had clearly passed during the hours of darkness; they cautiously opting not to travel along the broken trails and trekking overland both night and day to come to this point.

They were quite overjoyed when I made myself known to them, regaling me (through Thomas' translation) with tales of the horrors they had faced in the wild and inhospitable bush, and of their relief in finding me unharmed and their thankfulness for the cover I had provided in helping them to escape our attackers. For my part, I was overjoyed to see that Robert still carried not only his spear but the Horace-Wilkershire's winding tool; though I was less pleased to discover that the other two men were reduced to a handful of cartridges apiece for their Nitro Express rifles. The trio were, understandably, quite famished, and I confess that I felt a small twinge of hunger myself, so I bade them to stay put and quiet while I ventured off into the swelling morning light in hopes of procuring something for their supper (and obtaining a meal for myself in the process).

My men were more than happy to stay behind, exhausted as they were and, I think, a trifle cowed by the fact that they had fled and allowed a woman to cover their retreat. The terrain surrounding us was largely marked by scattered bush, from my height to twice that, and otherwise quite open. I hadn't gone a quarter of a mile when I encountered the first game, a giraffe cow and calf, stalking with an otherworldly self-possession and looking as alien as anything I had ever encountered. These were too large for my purposes, however, and would have provided more meat that we could consume or carry, as well as requiring that I use my rifle, which I was loathe to do with enemies still perhaps in earshot.

Shortly thereafter, however, I spied a graceful motion behind a line of thorn trees to my right and, creeping closer, soon determined its makers to be a small herd of impala, as red as an English deer on top and white bellied below, but my size or smaller, the males marked by great, upward and outward sweeping ringed horns. This was a far more appropriate prey so, placing my Gibbs and other loose items under a bush where I couldn't help but locate them later, I undertook a stalk.

When I rushed among them, though, their quick startle and great, pronking leaps left me feeling awkward and slow. I persevered, however, and after chasing the now scattered group for some hundreds of yards eventually came to understand the rhythm of their flight. When a pretty little doe leapt, stiff-legged and high to my right, then, I was ready and, pivoting, matched her spring. Things that rise will often converge, and thus we did, I wrapping her in my arms and making sure that, when we met the hard-packed earth together, she was below and I atop. As the doe kicked beneath me, I grasped her soft muzzle in one hand, stretched out the elegant length of her neck, and fed.

I had almost finished this welcome (if savorless) repast when I caught a motion from the corner of my eye. I was on my feet in an instant, scrambling back for my rifle and other possibles, and returned to encounter a creature out of a tawdry fiction nightmare. He was only twenty yards from me, having materialized out of the brush. If the fact that he had come so close without my knowledge did not reveal his nature, his feeding teeth, fully extended, answered all questions. He was tall, thin as a whip, with wide-set almost pointed ears, a crushed-flat nose, and eyes the yellow of a suppurating wound. I quickly covered him with the pepper-box, confident in the silver-and-oaken-bulleted round that was always first in that weapon's chamber, and waited for him to make a move.

He had seen me feeding, and clearly knew my nature as well as I his. Back hunched, and one string-muscled arm hanging loosely, he gestured with the other; first to the antelope which, in its last throes was stirring dust with its dainty hooves, and then to his own fanged mouth. Keeping him covered, I waved my other arm, hand open in what I thought to be a universal gesture of acquiescence, toward the impala. My uninvited guest clearly understood this crude pantomime, and fell upon the creature like a street cur on a dropped bun, slurping and growling in the back of his throat until the doe was quite still and clearly drained.

Trying my luck further, I waved him away, picked up the carcass and easily slung it over my shoulder and, pointing at him, and then in the direction from which I had come, bid him follow. To my relief and surprise he did so, though I kept the pepper-box in hand, and a wary eye upon him, until we arrived at the spot where my men waited.

Their glee at the sight of the impala on my shoulders soon changed to superstitious dread as they saw my strange companion; for though his teeth were likely not visible at such a distance, there was something unmistakably *other* about him that the trio immediately perceived. This proved fortunate, for I believe it quite drove any questions about how the antelope had died from their minds. Speaking to Thomas, and bidding him to translate, I explained that I believed the creature to pose no immediate danger, and that I was eager to gather some information from him.

We soon learned that our new companion spoke Matabele, being of that blood but owning no allegiance to any of Lobengula's Indunas, or priest-generals. There were others of his kind, it seemed, who lived apart from, and largely invisible to, the followers of the African Despot. He, separated from his kin and starving, had attempted to bring down a waterbuck, which had shattered his arm and, being too poor in blood to heal it rapidly, he had been facing a slow climb back to health on the energy of insect and rodent before he'd happened upon me in the bush.

This strange tale did nothing to alleviate the concerns of my party, but I had Thomas promise the creature, who claimed the name Shaka, after one of the Great Men of his tribal past, that we would provide him with sustenance if he would guide us to his village and assist us in parley with the inhabitants thereof. Shaka consented to this, clearly grateful for his deliverance, and exhibited remarkable self-control, only looking on longingly as my horse Melissa arrived in camp, having made her own miraculous escape and apparently following our trail for reasons of her own, unknowable to kin or man.

After Thomas had built a small dry-wood fire, the better to reduce tattle-tale smoke, my men all thoroughly discussed a hearty meal of impala chops. The creature Shaka and I did not partake, of course, though I made a good effort to appear to enjoy a cup of tea, courtesy of a my solar teapot and a cup that were among the few items Thomas had thought to rescue before fleeing camp.

All fed and watered, then, with dusk falling and my Coilcycle wound tight by an enthusiastic Robert, we continued along our intended route. Shaka ran easily alongside my Horace-Wilkershire, which seemed to neither amaze nor frighten him, while my three men took turns availing themselves of Melissa's saddle, behind which the rest of the impala and what little gear we had were also stowed.

We proceeded in this manner, keeping to the schedule I had previously established, for two days. In the absence of a tent, I was able to make use of a pair of tarpaulins that my horse had unwittingly carried to us, these being tied to her saddle in anticipation of wrapping materials for transport. They formed a reasonable daylight shelter in which I could sleep, and maintain my illusion of dining in private.

Shaka's hunger had begun to manifest itself in his every glance at man and horse, but I, through vague translation, urged him to patience, as I had no wish to slow our progress to hunt fresh game, nor to allow my men to become more thoroughly wary of him than they already were. In retrospect, I imagine they knew full well what he was (and perhaps what I was as well), but were loyal souls at heart, and determined to play out the hands they had bid upon come what may.

As we set out on the evening of the second day I heard voices in the distance, and soon was able to make out a group of mounted figures moving across the brush-broken side of a kopje, or hill, a half mile ahead. Knowing that the Matabele were loath to ride, I was quite certain that this cavalry was made up of either Englishmen or Dutch Boers, and moved to intercept them.

The party consisted of, as I discovered in short and gleeful order, Mr. Selous and a number of his volunteer Rangers, we having unwittingly intercepted them at almost precisely the point planned. Thus concluded a small enough adventure for me, but one which would have great implications as the struggle for Matabele-land continued.

CHAPTER 8

The Great Hunter seeks redress—A manhunt—A collar for Shaka—A trail of unmentionables--Raiding party sighted!—My vampire puts them to flight—A joyless victory.

Upon learning the details of our recent difficulties, Mr. Selous at once determined that we must set things to rights, and accordingly selected a dozen of his sturdiest riders to pursue and punish the Matabele raiding party, and recover what remained of our purloined possessions. I managed, with some difficulty, to secure a place among this group, with Selous' support overriding concerns about a woman accompanying the party and suspicions regarding my Coilcycle's ability to keep pace with their tried and true hunting ponies.

More problematic was Shaka, who became visibly excited as our plans were translated. I urged Thomas to bring him aside, and quickly learned, as I'd expected, that he was eager to take part in the attack, if only to satisfy his hunger. Explaining the situation to Selous, with, I assure you, some trepidation and no little use of euphemism, I pointed out that it would be useful to the furtherance of Mr. Rhodes' plans to gauge the effect Shaka had on the enemy, while admitting that his actions might spark superstitious terrors among our own men. The Great Hunter studied me in silence for a while, and I, whom had dared the gaze of elders of my kind, was hard put to resist squirming under that blue-eyed attention.

When he spoke, it was with a quiet confidence.

"These men have raised farms and families out of the unforgiving bush, my dear Miss Monot," he said. "They are not likely to be shocked by strange sights, and if they see your protégé engaging the Matabele bravely I believe they will cheer his efforts, whatever they consist of. Prudence, however, dictates that we devise some means by which they can identify him quickly in the melee, so ally does not unwittingly turn against ally."

Rummaging through my scant remaining luggage, I produced a bright yellow silk scarf, which I tied around Shaka's neck, much to his apparent delight. With our human hunting hound thus distinctively collared, we were ready to encounter our foes.

The rest of the camp was soon laagered up to wait for our return, and well defended in case of difficulties. Thomas, Michael and Robert were instructed to remain, despite their protestations, since none of them had any affinity for horses; as evidenced by their efforts to ride Melissa, which amounted to perching precariously atop her back while that worthy animal picked out the trail at her own measured pace.

The safari's security assured, we rode out and quickly picked up the raiding party's trail. In addition to dust beaten flat by bare feet, their progress was marked with goods examined and discarded. That these included a number of my under-things caused me no little embarrassment, and seemed to infuriate my companions. Many of these volunteers had, of course, come from remote farmsteads, where they had left wives and daughters, to join Selous in fighting the Savage King's hordes. Undoubtedly the sight of a Western woman's lace trampled into the dust of Africa brought unpleasant images to their minds, thoughts that did not, I reckoned, bode well for the raiders ahead of us.

In this I was not mistaken. Some few moments later we caught sight of our quarry, moving in undisciplined formation up the side of a distant kopje, looking for all the world like ants ascending a hill en route to the entrance to their home. No such sanctuary was in offering, however. Selous gave the command to attack, and I was quickly comforted to learn that my Horace-Wilkershire had no trouble pacing the salted horses in their rush and weave through the low and scattered thorn brush. The enemy of course took to their heels at the sound of hoof beats, but the relatively open country worked against their efforts, and it seemed we would soon be among them.

There were still a few Martini-Henrys and antique muzzle-loaders in our foes' possession, though most were armed only with assegais, knobkerries, and shields. Still, they prepared to make good use of what cover the terrain offered, and it looked like we were in for a war of attrition in our efforts to dislodge them. I had underestimated Shaka, though. With a howl of hunger he rushed forward, quite ignoring the swarm of weapons arrayed against him, and bowled over the nearest of the Matabele warriors, tearing his throat with a single savage bite and locking his mouth to the resulting wound.

The enemy broke at the sight of this horror, and fled willy-nilly ahead of our charge. I was surprised to see that, after an initial panicked rifle volley that went universally high, the warriors offered no resistance and, indeed, soon seemed to despair of even the odds of flight. Many simply stopped and stood, waiting for a bullet dispatched with terribly accuracy by a charging horseman. I'm afraid my comrades' blood was up, and no quarter was given. I'm not proud to say that I myself murdered two with my pepper-box at close range, having thriftily transferred the special cartridge to my last barrel so as not to waste it on foes that simple lead would so effortlessly fell. There was no joy in so doing and no sense of triumph after; it was not a battle but an extermination.

Other than the items that had been scattered along the trail, and a few things broken out of ignorance or plain bloody-mindedness, we were able to recover our gear in relatively good order. I was particularly gratified to discover unopened several crates of goods containing items I hoped to use in negotiating with the African kin. Loading these and our other supplies onto the recaptured oxen (the cart having been put to the torch by our enemies), we headed back to camp victorious, Shaka trotting happily beside my Cycle, his arm already knitting and his face and yellow scarf still sticky with Matabele blood. The operation had been a success on many levels but, in my case at least, it left me victim to a vague unease, and much regretting that such slaughter had not offered *me* an opportunity to feed.

CHAPTER 9

Back in camp—The chivalry of Selous—Not exactly a bible—Not exactly a communion—A touch of intimacy.

We settled into our laagered camp on return, and I was shown to a tent that had been erected for my comfort. I took my dinner of tea, hard bread, and antelope steak into its privacy, as was my custom, the better to continue the illusion that I ate as the others did. I was ruminating upon how to best dispose of the food, my concentration splintered by my growing hunger, when I heard Selous calling to me from without.

"Miss Monot," he said. "Are you in a condition to permit my entry?"

I pushed the plate aside, disturbing its contents to make it appear to others in the safari as if I had been eating, and bade him come in. This he did, slouch hat in one hand, and carefully leaving the tent flap open to allay any suspicions that might cloud his or my reputation. He glanced at the plate and, squatting easily on his heels, spoke in a whisper.

"Might I be frank, Miss?" he began.

I nodded my assent, and he continued.

"I have a confession to make," he said. "Holmes and Rhodes have confided quite completely in me about both your mission and your nature. I am concerned about your strength for the travails ahead, and offer my assistance if it would be of help to you."

I studied his strange eyes, searching for any duplicity there, and finally whispered, my head bent in thanks.

"It would. I am hungry to the point of weakness. But how would you propose we accomplish this in the midst of such a busy camp?"

I saw something akin to fear in his face, then, the first and only time I ever did so, but he continued without the slightest break in his voice.

"Have you a Bible, miss? I thought perhaps if it were to appear that we prayed together, I might offer you the succor of my wrist."

Here I blushed, for I had no such volume. Digging through my recovered property, however, I was able to offer a copy of Mr. Twain's *The American Claimant*, which that worthy author had recently written with the aid of the miracle of phonographic dictation.

The Hunter laughed softly.

"At least the cover is black," he said, "and that will make it Bible enough to any who pass by. Place it open on the table, and allow me to kneel beside you in an attitude of study."

I did so, and as he read aloud from it, giving the light prose the weight of scripture, I accepted his offered wrist, and noted that his voice did not break in the slightest as my feeding teeth pieced it, nor as I bowed my own head to this welcome feast, in as close to an attitude of prayer as my kind ever achieves.

The act of feeding is, of course, intimate and erotic to both participants, and it was all I could do to maintain my demure posture through the process. When I had finished, I noted that Selous' voice had become the slightest bit heavy-breathed, as well. He rolled his sleeve over the wound, already healing thanks to the miraculous benefits of kindred saliva, and rose, only very slightly unsteady, to his feet. I looked up at him then, and, lowering my glasses on my nose, gave him the full measure of my neonate gaze.

"Thank you, sir; I am comforted as if by prayer."

He held my glance for some moments, and I believe for once he found my eyes as disconcerting as I had his.

"There is no need for blasphemy, surely. It was a...it was a pleasure, Miss Monot." He said. "I hope we have occasion to read together again soon."

Selous slipped out then, letting the tent flap fall upon my privacy. I studied its rough weave long after he had departed, my mind traveling paths that neither the good book of the Christians nor the humorous musings of Mr. Twain would have sent it careening along.

CHAPTER 10

We split our party—Following Shaka's lead—The Coilcycle's prowess—A buffalo stampede!—Trapped beneath my machine—The Hunter rescues me—A scent I will profit by remembering.

With our goods, or the greater part of them at least, now recovered; and Shaka in our company, it was imperative that we return to our original mission. After some consultation with Selous, we determined that the main body of his force, under the command of the Boer Captain Van Niekerk of the Afrikaner Corps and including our recaptured oxen, would press deeper into Matabele-land in hopes of determining the enemy's positions of strength and perhaps drawing the attention of its Impis.

Though Van Niekerk's party was small, the wily farmer/warrior was confident that, if he could lure his foes into giving chase, he could inflict significant damage while emerging largely unscathed. And, of course, such activity would make it easier for my little group, consisting of myself, Selous, Shaka, Thomas, Michael, and Robert, to safely follow the African vampire's lead in an attempt to make contact with his people. It was thought that our smaller party would be less likely to either inflame or frighten Shaka's people, and that his affiliation with us, coupled with my own nature (though this was not discussed aloud) would provide us with the credentials to open a conversation. (And did I wonder how many other reasons the Great Hunter had for aligning himself with my group? Most certainly I did.)

The decision made, we soon went our separate ways. Our new ally seemed eager enough to take us to his people's stronghold and, though I suspect some in my little party feared that we were jumping from the pan into the fire, as it were, I was cautiously confident that some sort of rough alliance could be formed with these fierce creatures who were after all, however distant, kin of mine.

Initially we moved though mixed scrub country, relatively open and distinguished by a crusted, sandy soil. Shaka hounded ahead, quite healed now and strong with new blood, and seemingly in a hurry to rejoin his tribe. Selous followed, his hunting pony easily picking its way, slack reined, around the small acacias and tangles of wait-a-bit thorn. I kept my Coilcycle to the more trodden paths to prevent its wheels sinking through the crust and laboring in the sand beneath, riding my brakes so as to not outrun my companions, and occasionally rising to stand on the foot-pegs for greater balance as I maneuvered it around the rare tighter bits of brush. Melissa bore our gear in bags strapped across her saddle, while Thomas, Michael, and Robert relied upon Shank's mare; the experience of horseback riding having made a less than favorable impression on their unaccustomed backsides.

Though our progress was largely without incident of note, I will describe one experience that might prove of interest to students of natural history, and that will loom large later in this narrative. We were travelling down the middle of a river bed, some thirty yards wide and completely dry (though its high banks gave testimony to how wildly it might run, however briefly, in the rainy season). Without brush and largely level and firm of surface, it made for a convenient highway as long as its course matched our own.

Thomas was aware of the danger first, and spoke quickly to Selous in the MaShona tongue. The hunter comprehended our situation immediately.

"Make for the bank, Miss Monot," he shouted, turning his horse. "Something has stampeded a herd of Cape buffalo behind us, and in moments this channel will be a veritable river of hoofed and horned death."

I arrived at the edge of river bed with the others, but paused there looking for a more gradual rise up which I could ride my Coilcycle. Melissa scrambled up the bank easily, as did Selous' pony and of course my crew; Shaka in particular scaling it with all the agility of a spider, his arm quite healed. I could hear the herd now, like an earthquake that is apparent to the ears in the moments before the ground begins to move.

"Leave the machine, Miss Monot, and climb!" Selous ordered. But I did not like the thought of abandoning my Cycle and so, standing on the pegs to put my weight closer to the handlebars, I selected a possible avenue of ascent and urged the machine forward.

I nearly made it, too, only to find, within inches of clearing the rim, my front wheel climbing up and back, its knobbed tire pawing at the air. In a moment the Cycle flipped, pinning me beneath it in the river bed. The sound of hooves, and the panicked bovine calling of the herd, seemed almost upon me.

I struggled to extricate myself from my trap, and would surely soon have done so, but found the burden suddenly flung from me and hands roughly dragging me up the bank. Selous dropped me there and, with an appraising glance at the herd now only yards distant, leapt down again and propped my Cycle securely against the edge of the river bed before scrambling to safely himself as the vanguard thundered past, wild eyed and smelling like an American cattle drive.

We huddled there as the great herd rushed by. Selous, ever the Hunter, remarked upon the particularly broad sweep of horn displayed by several of the bulls. It seemed long minutes before the great, black river of buffalo had passed, though it was likely a far shorter period of time. Once it had, we removed ourselves to the river bed and proceeded in the animals' wake, the air thick with dust and the ground as littered with and redolent of manure as any barnyard

CHAPTER II

*Camp by a waterhole—Standing watch with Selous—
Further intimacies—My wiles employed—Signs of
things to come?*

On the third day of our explorations, our little party made camp for the heat of the day beneath a large baobab tree close to a rapidly drying water hole. Though the liquid remaining had been so stirred by thirsty beasts that it was mud-brown and had the consistency of cream, when strained through a blanket (for my filter had been lost to the Matabele, and would not at any rate have proved capable of dealing with such mud) it produced a tea that seemed to meet with approval of our group.

I, of course, only made show of sipping the concoction before slipping into the solitude of my tent. It was there, as the sun dipped low into the brief color-splash of African twilight, that Selous approached me again, coughing politely from without so that I could bid him enter.

"Your men are weary, Miss Monot," he said, an unlikely nervousness apparent in his voice. "And Shaka's agitation leads me to believe we are not far from our destination. I would prefer we were quite at our best when we arrive there. Would you perhaps join me in standing watch from the hillock to the west while we allow our party a bit more rest before moving on?"

I quickly assented, sensing the real intent beneath the Hunter's words and, with his instructions translated to our small group (all of whom, save the eager vampire, were clearly glad for the additional break), Selous and I set off on foot for the sentry post he had selected. He took the lead, his Gibbs balanced easily on his shoulder, the barrel held in his right hand. By the time we reached the hill the winking tropical twilight had passed, and the full darkness of African night had fallen as decisively as a theatrical curtain.

The Hunter spread a rough blanket on the ground and we sat. The silence hung heavy for some moments as I, fair trembling with hunger and a decidedly separate but no less delicious form of anticipation, waited for him to speak.

This he soon did, while unbuttoning one khaki cuff and shucking his sleeve back to reveal his wrist.

"I believe you are in need of restoration as well, Miss?" he said, carefully avoiding my eyes. "And I would not willingly face what lies ahead with you at less than full capacity. Of all our number, the success of our little escapade rests most firmly upon you."

I murmured my thanks, taking the proffered wrist in my left hand and raising it to my lips. As I did so I contrived to lean against him, my head on his shoulder, in the attitude of a maid cuddling with her beau as they share the light of the moon. Selous flinched briefly as I bit, letting out a gasp that more closely resembled a long-held breath released. As I fed, and as the intimacy of the act worked its will upon us both, he moved into my lean, and soon his free arm reached all tentative across my back to hold me close, his fingers splayed across my ribcage.

Quite emboldened by the eroticism of the experience, I contrived to turn my upper body, bringing his hand in contact with the swell of my bosom. The Great Hunter moaned more loudly at that encounter than he ever had at the touch of my teeth, but I was soon gratified to feel his fingers close over my breast with something akin to hunger.

I was aware that Selous was famous for his adherence to the Victorian ideal of morality, but found no shortage of rationalizations for my actions in our lonely distance from civilization and the precarious nature of our enterprise. Feeding still, I dared my hand to the front of his trousers and, with a quick and wicked manipulation of his buttons, freed his gratifyingly swollen member to the night air.

"Miss Monot," he began, but we both, I think, knew that the time for hesitation had escaped us. Indeed, before I had administered many caresses he spent himself quite explosively, staining the blanket upon which we sat and spilling hot seed upon my hand.

When I lifted my mouth from his wrist, the Hunter turned his back to me as he refastened his breeches. For my part, I cleaned my fingers upon the blanket, confident that this and the earlier besmirching would be lost among the many indignities that rough cloth had endured during our time on the trail. As we collected our belongings to return to camp, I contemplated offering an apology for my bawdiness. I determined, however, that we had set upon a path that would offer ample opportunities for the expression of regret, and followed my Champion to the campfires feeling quite refreshed and, I confess, not a little smug.

CHAPTER 12

Shaka takes us home—The African kin—Not a warm welcome—Taken to the Induna—A remarkable woman—My patience tried too far—Interview with the vampire Priestess—She bids me to unclothe myself--Gifts great and small—A difficult negotiations—No alliance, but freedom.

The following evening, with the setting sun briefly tangled in the limbs of a distant acacia tree, we broke camp for what promised to be the final leg of this phase of our adventure. Shaka took the lead, of course, ranging eagerly ahead like a hound on a scent. Selous followed the creature closely, his Gibbs secure in a saddle scabbard, and his bright eyes diving deep into every night-thickened shadow and tangle of brush. I at one point tried to ride up to him (the pace being no impediment to my Coilcycle), but the Great Hunter, perhaps still feeling awkward in the aftermath of our little adventure the evening before, warned me off with the palm of his hand.

Somewhat chastened, I fell back to take up the vanguard for the rest of our party, inwardly vowing, nevertheless, to remain close enough to the fore to assume command of the situation should contact with my African kin indeed be established.

It being a clear night, and the moon waxing gibbous, we were able to maintain a respectable pace despite the lateness of evening. We had not so journeyed too many miles when our erstwhile tracker suddenly dropped to his knees and turned his head to one side, exposing his throat in something of the manner of a cur expressing subordination.

Quickly settling my Coilcycle on its kick stand, I rushed to Shaka's side, the better to let those who observed us (and I was confident that we were being so studied, though neither Selous nor I had yet been able to espy any movement in the terrain ahead) note the fluidity of my movement and thus discern my nature.

I believe I saw our welcoming party before the Hunter did (and I confess that I indulged in a bit of self-satisfaction as a result, despite the dangers inherent in our situation). There were perhaps a dozen of them, male and female, quite naked save for scraps of bark or commandeered cloth hanging over their loins. They were whip-thin all, knob-jointed with strap-like muscles clearly delineated beneath their skin. They could have been particularly benighted examples of *Homo sapiens*, but for their inhuman grace and the fact that, to a man, their feeding teeth were erect and their eyes betrayed a ferocious hunger.

Standing next to the now trembling Shaka, I showed no subservience, but let my own teeth slip free from my gums and waved the obviously terrified Thomas forward to translate. My days of masquerading as human had run their course.

The creatures before me were for the most part unarmed (and why, indeed, would they have need of such?), though a few did carry assegais and crude knives, likely spoils stripped from the corpses of their victims. They seemed at first at a loss as to what to make of me, which allowed me time to stiffen Thomas' spine with some choice words before I endeavored to speak to my wild kin. When I judged that my major domo was quite up to the task, I began.

"Greetings," I said, "as you can see I am like you, though my skin is pale and my hair yellow. I come from a place many days travel from here, a place where such as we are common. I have come to speak to he or she who leads you, to offer gifts and to bring doom down upon our mutual enemies."

Some discussion followed my little speech, and disagreement was evident in their raised voices and sometimes wild gesticulations, but eventually a woman stepped forward from among them and spoke.

"We hear your words, blood sister," she said, (though Thomas stumbled with the last, as the term was apparently foreign to him, and thus I can assume it is at best an approximate translation). "We will take you to our Induna, and she shall weigh the worth of your presents and the truth of your promises."

With that the entire group turned as one and melted with uncanny silence into the night ahead of us, with Shaka bounding after them and looking like nothing so much as an eager puppy. I hurried to my Coilcycle to follow, noting with some surprise that my little entourage seemed singularly untroubled by the fact that I had publicly revealed my nature. I thought briefly of the many chops buried beneath the sand of my tents, and all my other wasted subterfuges; but I realized also that Selous had not drawn his Gibbs from its saddle holster during the entire affair and, buoyed by this unspoken affirmation of his confidence in me, urged my party forward with a wave of my hand and followed the wraiths into the darkness.

In a little less than an hour I detected the familiar sweet scent of wood smoke on the air, and shortly thereafter was able to make out the faint yellow dance of a series of fires through the brush before us. We followed out hosts (with Shaka close at their heels) into a large clearing lit by a series of blazes and marked by an assortment of thatch huts of the crudest imaginable nature.

There Shaka turned and bid us stop, with frantic hand gestures and a high-pitched plea so warped by nervousness that Thomas was at a loss to decipher anything beyond its central message. We did so; with the interpreter, our "pet," and I to the fore (I had slipped from my Cycle again as soon as we'd been so urgently asked to stop); and the Great Hunter (himself unhorsed out of courtesy, but with his rifle casually held over his shoulder, gripped by the barrel), Michael, and Robert a few steps behind.

We waited thus for some minutes, whilst curious faces appeared and as suddenly disappeared in the doorways of the thatched hovels, and then—to the accompaniment of a steady drumming of spear butts on the hard earth by her retinue, the Induna (for I certainly assumed it was she) appeared at the far end of the encampment and approached us.

She was tall even in comparison to her people, easily six feet in height, and possessed a regal bearing and a peculiar pared-down beauty. Her face was long, her eyes almost catlike (approaching even those characteristic of individuals of the Oriental persuasion). Like the others, she wore only a loincloth, and her form was so thin that it appeared stripped to the essence, proving that a human being can find favor in the eyes of others even if reduced to no more than skin and bone, sinew and hard slats of muscle. Her head was shaved, as were her eyebrows, and, like all of her people, she wore her feeding teeth fully exposed, as if proudly refusing to bow to the prejudices of the world.

This remarkable creature was accompanied by six others, whom I took to be her chief advisors, divided equally between the genders. Each carried a spear of Metabele manufacture (certainly, I now decided, the spoils of war) with which they pounded the earth in perfect unison with her every stately step.

Though Shaka now abased himself with forehead to the ground, and Thomas trembled head to toe as if he were about to bolt, I drew myself up to my modest height and, through the filters of my tinted glasses daring to look the apparition in the eyes despite my neonate status, bade my interpreter to translate as I repeated the greeting I had tendered before.

The Induna's party remained quiet until Thomas had finished this chore, at which point one of her male advisers let out a howl of anger and jumped between his mistress and I, gesticulating wildly and screaming words which, though my cowering major domo was too overcome to put into English for me, certainly did not seem to bode well for me or my followers.

Worse still, this seemed but the beginnings of a performance most dramatic indeed. Soon he was dancing immediately in front of me, drumming the earth with his horny soles and thrusting his spear at me in mock combat. I quickly realized that his motions with that weapon would appear to be superhumanly fast to my followers (and, in fact, they were), and that to a man (save Selous, of course) they were on the brink of panic.

And so, timing my opponent's movements nicely (and counting upon the overconfidence that soon became quite apparent in his display), I used my own not inconsiderable speed and dexterity to pluck the spear from him in mid-thrust, spin it in my hands and drive the rounded wooden butt of it into his emaciated midsection. This caused him to let out an "oof!" of surprise and land upon his bottom in the dust in a manner quite comical.

Indeed, there were titters of humor from my party, and even some corresponding smiles among the Induna's group.

These, and perhaps his own humiliation at being so bested, were more than the poor creature could take. Scrambling to his feet, he flung himself at me, his face a mask of fury, fanged mouth wide, and fingers curled into grasping claws.

I made ready to receive his assault, but had not cleared my pepperbox from its pocket when my enemy came to a sudden standstill. As casually as a debutante turning a page in the latest novel, the Induna had reached out and grabbed my assailant by the back of the neck. She held him there effortlessly for a moment and then, her strange eyes on my own, closed her long fingers around his throat until he bucked and choked and trembled and went still, to the horror of his party and mine.

I realized at once that she must have crushed his spine in her thin fingers, effectively pinching off the connection between head and body; simple asphyxiation would not have ended such a resilient creature. I wondered at the strength required to do such damage so casually, and at the iron will that would allow her to do so without hesitation. I steeled myself, however, and tried to match the Induna's nonchalance as I awaited her reply.

It soon became apparent, however, that she had little to say for the moment. Instead, she circled me slowly, sticklike fingers touching in turn my hair and my clothing, for all the world as if determining what constituted my actual form and which was merely covering. After circumnavigating me once completely, she paused again, drew her hands down her own nearly naked form and, pointing at me and flicking her fingers in a dismissive gesture, spoke a single guttural word.

I turned to Thomas for elucidation, but that worthy seemed tongue-tied and unwilling to convey her message to me. I had understood the sign language clearly enough, however, and took the burden of disclosure from him.

"She wishes me to unclothe myself, does she not?" I asked, striving for calm.

Selous exclaimed with indignation, "Miss Monot, surely you mustn't!"

"On the contrary, my dear Hunter," I replied, "it appears that I must." (I should explain here that, whatever trepidation I might have had of unclothing myself in this situation, I was certainly not concerned that I would excite the carnal appetites of either my crew or our vampiric hosts. Truth be told, these are societies in which nakedness is far more the norm than in ours--witness the Induna who was facing me, for example--and I suspected that if anything I would appear less "other" to them were I to face them *au natural.* I also realized, of course, that Selous had no such societal familiarity to fall back on, and I do confess to a wicked tingle of pleasure as I contemplated the effects my naked body--of which I was appropriately, I think, proud-- might have on his carefully maintained stoicism.)

Certainly most women of our Age would be horrified at the thought of such a public disrobing, but I considered myself a Modern Female and, given the precarious of our situation, determined to shuck off my clothing as casually as possible, though not without some difficulty due to the complexity of costumes of the time. Noting that the Induna did sport a loincloth, I decided to draw the line at my pantalettes, which indulgence she seemed of a mind to grant me.

Though I was not particularly shy and, as I've already noted, had no fear of rapacious consequences, I did worry that I would be shedding a certain mystery, and thus a crude magic, along with my clothing. To counter this, I made every effort to hold the Induna's gaze as I stripped. In truth this was extremely difficult, for though her eyes were yellow and bloodshot, she was clearly a far older creature than I and, had she wanted (or dared), could, I believe, have commanded me with the force of her glance alone. That she did not do so may have been due to her own uncertainties concerning my power, strange entity that I must have seemed to her. Or, perhaps, my tinted glasses (which I had not doffed) might have confused her. It could also, I must admit, have been due to a capacity for kindness that, though often present, we hesitate to attribute to our more primitive cousins.

After the Induna has studied me carefully, circling me again but this time refraining from any touch, she indicated with a nod that I might clothe myself. I did so, again fumbling somewhat with the more complex of my garments but careful to not appear hurried lest I give a clue to my discomfort (for however Modern I considered myself, it was an extraordinarily disconcerting position I found myself in). As I did I was amused to hear a sigh, as if of relief, from my safari crew. Apparently, far from being inflaming, my near nakedness had been an uncomfortable if not disturbing sight. A glance over my shoulder told me that the chivalrous Hunter, though exposed to no more than my bare limbs and back, had carefully averted his eyes. I shall always wonder if he weakened enough to steal a glance at some point during my ordeal.

I had little opportunity to dwell on these matters, however, for, with a few mumbled words, the Induna indicated a nearby hut. I turned to Thomas who confirmed what I already suspected.

"She says the sun is coming, mistress," he whispered, "and she wishes you to join her within."

I replied that I desired to keep my entourage near and, upon this being translated, she accepted the condition with what I interpreted as a wave of derision. Thus we two entered the enclosure, with Thomas squatting just beyond the door.

The interior of the structure was clean, its dirt floor clearly swept. The hut was dark and cool, and I determined that it would remain so through the heat of the day, with air entering by way of the portal and exiting via a number of cleverly situated vents along the eaves. I also noted that the earth nearest the walls was stained dark; apparently water was applied to the thatch when the sun was high to provide a measure of evaporative cooling.

Following my host's example, I seated myself upon a zebra skin on the floor and, with my major domo translating through another hide that covered the doorway, began my interview.

"Though you look like one of the white cattle," she began, her voice a gruff singsong, "you are clearly my sister. You have said that there are more of our kind where you come from. Explain."

I confess that I exaggerated somewhat our role in civilized society, implying that we were many and lived in a negotiated symbiosis with the warm blooded. I mentioned the names of Rhodes and indeed the English Queen, though neither sparked any recognition in her strange eyes. At that point I described the Mistress of the City, and presented the Induna with a gift which Lady Ellen had entrusted me; a necklace supporting a small vial which contained a few drops of that worthy's precious blood. The Priestess took it with some confusion, until I unscrewed the cap to better let her appreciate that which she had been gifted. Upon its opening the Induna sniffed eagerly, rolling her eyes back until only the yellowed whites showed and lifting her lips away from her teeth like a snuffling hound.

After so savoring the bouquet of Lady Ellen's gift for some moments, the creature recapped the bottle (effortlessly

I might add, though it is certain that she had never before encountered a screw cap, or a screw for that matter). Returning her eyes to their normal state, which was no less disturbing, she focused her attention upon me again.

"So I see now that our kin are not all as children in your land." She said, though "land" is an approximate translation, her understanding of the great world beyond her and the many peoples in it lacking. "What other presents do you bring to convince me to make treat with you and take your enemies as my own?"

I confess that I did not much like her tone, or the implication that I had come to her on bended knee. My alternatives, however, seemed limited, so I instructed Thomas (still shivering just beyond the door) to have the items which I had intended for trade and gift-giving brought forward. I cautioned him, however, to leave some of the poorer goods, and one chest of the better, behind, so as not to spend all my pence on breakfast and starve for want of supper.

That worthy accomplished the task in short order and, leaving two crates in the doorway, returned to his frightened station. Thomas was a strong man, yet had struggled bringing one container to us at a time. I was impressed, then, if not exactly surprised, to see the Induna heft one in each hand and set them before me on the dirt floor.

The chests contained a variety of goods, including items I had obtained in hope of engaging in trade with whatever rude cultures we might meet on our journey. As a result, they included no end of the sort of faux jewelry, knives, and iron tools I had planned to exchange with less exotic civilizations than the one I now found myself in. I had, of course, also anticipated my current situation, hence each crate contained a separate package designed (as best I could imagine from the far remove of the Civilized World's shopping districts) to appeal to my African kin.

It was these I unwrapped now for the appraisal of my hostess. The first contained an assortment of simple cotton tunics and drawstring trousers in muted browns and grays. For I had surmised that, however dark their skin, any like me would still suffer discomfort in the full light of the day and would benefit from such garments. The second consisted of packaged bundles of sulfur matches, and here I quite prided myself on my choice. Fire-making in primitive society is, after all, akin to magic, and often the province of a local person of influence quite apart from the ruler. By giving the Induna such capability, I hoped, I would be further cementing her grip upon power.

The clothing seemed to puzzle her at first, so I produced an artist's rendering of an individual dressed in such garments. She nodded her understanding then but, after a few moments of pawing through the bundle, tossed the contents aside and looked at me with an air of disappointment. I was disheartened by this apparent rejection but, soldiering on, slipped a single Lucifer from one of the packages and, flicking its tip with my fingernail, caused it to spark into flame.

Here the Induna's reaction was far more gratifying, for she stepped back involuntarily and voiced a low "ahhhh" of wonder and concern. I blew out the match and, presenting another to her, mimed the procedure for bringing it to life, using the dead head of the Lucifer I still held. After several attempts she was successful. And, though she threw the match to the floor immediately upon its lighting, her yellow eyes gleamed with avarice and she took the bundle from me and clutched it to her bony bosom.

However pleased she might have been by the offering, however, I was soon to learn that her greed was not yet sated. If I'd thought she was oblivious to my glasses, I was disabused of that notion as she reached out and snatched them from my face, the movement so rapid that I was unable to react. I glanced away quickly, but not before she was able to sense the power that the glasses had hidden (though I do not think she realized that their filtering worked in both directions, the simple tinting hiding what abilities I had while making me less susceptible to the strength of her own much more formidable gaze). I spoke quickly to maintain whatever advantage they'd left me.

"Ah, you have ruined my surprise, Priestess," I said, "but you shall have it nonetheless." Calling to Thomas, I bade him bring the last chest of barter goods forward. When he had done so, I lifted it into the hut (hinting at my own strength as I did so, though it was nothing like as heavy as the earlier boxes). Throwing open the lid, I found a leather case atop the more plebian trade goods, and unfastened its top to reveal several dozen pairs of glasses like my own, with blue-lenses and sporting elegant gold wire-rimmed frames, that I had purchased during my brief sojourn in Egypt.

Presenting them to the Induna, I was able to retrieve my own spectacles and, fitting them to my face, announced, "They will shield your eyes from the gaze of the midday sun, and disguise their strength until it is needed. It is a fitting gift, I think, for such a powerful ally."

The Induna toyed with the presents, opening and closing the earpieces and holding the tinted lenses to her own eyes, before she spoke.

"You have not bought my allegiance, little sister, but you have won your freedom. Despite the urging of my advisers, I shall grant you safe passage to the edges of our lands, if I only have your sworn word that you will not venture into the home territory of my people again."

I attempted to remonstrate, but no sooner had I begun to speak than she turned her back to me, signaling that the interview had concluded, and a brace of her lieutenants threw open the skin covering the door and pointed my way back to my people with rusted but still capable looking spears.

Rejoining my little safari, with Thomas close at my heels, I saw that a number of the remaining vampires had stationed themselves in twin lines, facing each other and scarcely more than a yard apart, to create a gauntlet leading us to the edge of the village. We made our way through it without incident, myself leading and Selous, his rifle in hand and ready, bringing up the rear.

It was only after we were in the clear that we heard shouts from the compound behind us and turned to see Shaka, a pair of thrown spears still trembling point first in the hard earth behind him, legging it toward us with quite a miraculous turn of speed.

"He insists that he join us," Thomas translated for the winded creature when he arrived. "He says he has a debt to you that he has not yet repaid."

I looked back toward where he had come and, seeing no signs of pursuit save the twin thrown spears, nodded my assent. So it was that our small party, all alive but bearing the heavy weight of failure on our shoulders, left the camp of the African vampires and faced the uncertain future that lay before us.

CHAPTER 13

A disappointed departure—Back to basics—Stalking the beautiful kudu—A crude but needed repast—Looking to an uncertain future.

When one's mission dismounts, necessity must ride, and so I determined to subdue my disappointment by procuring a supply of fresh meat for our little party. I soon made my intentions known to Selous and, though I suspect the Great Hunter would have preferred to see to such chores himself, I believe he recognized my need for the antiseptic of action and so agreed to my plan.

The first matter of business, of course, was to put some distance between ourselves and the village of our unwilling allies. My safari was all too eager to do so, and thus in relatively short order we had covered some miles and were established in a camp—thoroughly skermed with a fence of tightly woven thorn bush—adjacent to a game-soiled but usable waterhole.

From here I set forth alone, wishing to shoulder my disappointment in solitude. I determined it best to travel on foot, leaving my Coilcycle in camp, and carrying my Farquharson-action Gibbs. Self pity, I quickly found, is difficult to maintain while hunting, and soon the puzzles of animal tracks, cover, and winds fully occupied my mind, driving my angst in rout before them.

The waterhole acted as a center from which game trails radiated in every direction. So busy were these that it was difficult to worry out the spoor of one creature, but eventually I spied the distinctive heart-shaped print of what I presumed to be a kudu bull superimposed upon the comings and goings of the creatures that had trod the path before it. This I dedicated myself to following and, moving slowly at first (as winds had swept the more open portions of the trail, and the passing of smaller creatures occasionally superimposed themselves upon the tracks I pursued, at times quite obscuring them), soon lost myself in diligent pursuit.

I proceeded in this manner patiently, and as my gradual but steady progress took me ever closer to my quarry, so the prints became fresher and more easily identified. A bull kudu is a striking animal, with long spiraled horns, great expressive ears, and a distinctive coat, with bold white stripes against a blue-gray background. Though the size of a small horse, such an animal can, when remaining motionless behind the vertical lines of a thicket of bush, be all but invisible to the searching eye.

Thus did I approach too closely, my eyes on the trail rather than on my surroundings, and was only alerted to the beast's presence when my attention was captured by its bark of alarm, followed by the crashing of its bounding escape. Though I was quick to raise my Gibbs and snuggle my cheek against the stock, the shot was an uncertain one and, lowering the rifle, I took to my heels in pursuit.

It was here that I found full redemption, in the joy of pursuing a fast and agile prey. As I stretched my legs, jinking when the bull veered brd leaping the low bushes he leapt, I felt purged of disappointment and full again of the determination and optimism that had so far fueled my quest.

Eventually the pace told on the brave creature and, frothed and trembling, unable to flee further, he turned broadside to me. Even in such straights the kudu made no move to come to terms with his heartless pursuer, the species being by nature a timid and gentle antelope. Flush with excitement, I was tempted to leap upon its back and settle the matter with my own hands and teeth, but wisdom held sway as, even exhausted and panicked, the beast was large enough to do me such damage with hoof and horn that I would have cause to regret.

Thus I raised the Gibbs and, taking a moment to bring my breath under control, sighted carefully and shot the bull through the heart. Upon receiving the bullet, it started into a headlong run and, after charging recklessly in this manner for some one-hundred yards, its front legs giving way first and triggering a dramatic cartwheel, it was already dying as it hit the ground.

Knowing that the sound of the shot would carry to our camp, and that I should soon have company (my crew eager for the fresh meat and Selous, or at least so I fantasized, motivated by his concern for my safety), I partook of a quick meal of the crude and cooling blood and sat, leaning against the surprisingly sweet-smelling carcass (as redolent of flowered pasture as the hide of any pampered dairy cow), to await the arrival of my companions.

Cutting the kudu up and setting the bulk of the meat to dry in the shade (while my crew and indeed Selous roasted morsels of the back-strap and other select delicacies over a small fire) occupied the remainder of the day. And so it was well fed, and somewhat relieved of the dark clouds that had pursued us in our flight from the village of the African vampires, that the Famous Hunter and I set our minds to the future and how we might still serve the needs of our mutual benefactors.

CHAPTER 14

Alternatives considered—A bold gamble suggested—Shaka admits there are others--We determine to search for the "less than"–Forewarnings ignored—A dangerous journey begun.

"We might take the battle to Lobengula's armies directly," I offered. "We are few, I concede, but the leaders of the Impis know you and fear you; and I believe that Shaka and I, though only two, would provide a disproportionate influence through surprise and superstitious dread."

Selous appeared to consider my words, all the while using a knife to shape a bit of wart-hog ivory into what would eventually be a white bead for the front of his Gibbs to facilitate sighting in poor light.

"That is certainly an option, Miss Monot," he eventually replied, eyes on his work and not, I noticed with some petulance, upon myself. "But I move that we consider it our final alternative, and not accept its inevitability quite so soon." Here he held the little ball of ivory between thumb and forefinger and examined it carefully before resuming work.

"I believe," he continued, "though I do not pretend to be an expert in such matters, that the population of your *people* is less than united in many places where you are found, and far from monolithic even in England. Is this true, my lady?"

70

I was unsure of the ultimate unraveling of this conversational thread and, though the Hunter had certainly been made aware of our existence by creatures far wiser than me, I remained hesitant to lift the curtain too far and thus reveal things that were better kept secret.

"In this we are not unlike any nationality or society, dear Frederick," and I noted with perverse pleasure how he flinched at the term of endearment and my presumptive use of his given name, "we have our social strata, our guilds, and our royalty."

"And even your wars, I believe?" Here he dared my eyes, and I in turn was reminded again of the power his own, clear and bright and beautifully blue. I'm ashamed to say I broke that glance before he did.

"And even our wars, yes," I replied softly.

"Why then," he continued, warming to his argument, "do we assume that Shaka's tribe is alone among your peers in this country? Is it not possible that there are other such groups and that, though we have spent most of our trade goods, you might still be able to bring about an alliance through your charm and wit alone?"

The compliment was prettily delivered, and I was once again glad that a blush, among my kind, was more commonly a learned and practiced rather than an automatic response. I withheld mine with some effort, as deliberately as one might move a chess piece.

Still, the logic of the Hunter's conjecture quite startled me, and I chastised myself silently for, in the throes of my disappointment, not having considered such a possibility myself. That chagrin was quickly quite overwhelmed, however, with the excitement that came with the realization that we might still achieve our original objectives.

Complimenting the Legendary Naturalist on his wisdom, in short order I called Thomas to us and bade him to bring

Shaka to where we sat (as the African vampire, though he had earned the respect of all in battle, was still not exactly welcome among my other boys), and to be prepared to provide translation while we questioned the creature. (For, though Selous spoke the language of the Matabele, I hoped Thomas' greater fluency might be useful in the discussion of such a delicate subject.)

This my major domo soon did, with my African kin trotting at his heels, clearly as excited as a child to be so singled out for attention.

"Tell him we are grateful that he has chosen to accompany us," I instructed Thomas. "And then ask him if there be any others like him, apart from those in the village from which he comes." I knew the query had struck home because, upon hearing it, Shaka trembled, and was unable to keep his eyes upon us, and gave every sign of extreme discomfort, but spoke not a word.

"Make it clear that I need to know, Thomas," I urged, lowering my glasses and giving the vampire the limited force of my neonate eyes (for though I was no match for his Induna, all of his kin were not so formidable), "tell him that, should he have this knowledge and keep it from me, I will be most unhappy with him."

Upon hearing this tears actually flowed from the poor vampire's eyes and he dropped to his knees, striking his forehead on the ground quite forcefully three times, before replying in a tremulous voice.

"There are such creatures, my queen," or so at least Thomas interpreted the title bestowed upon me. "But they are far from here and they are not like you and I, they are..." Here my translator was apparently at a loss to come up with an English equivalent. He finally settled on an approximation. "They are *less than.*"

The excitement of suddenly spotting your game after a long and intricate stalk has nothing upon the thrill I felt at this confession.

"He must take us to them, Thomas. Tell him this. Tell him that when he does so he will be rewarded handsomely, however our encounter with these less-than creatures might conclude."

Shaka cringed as if struck with a sjambok whip at this command, and replied with a rapid delivery of syllables.

"He says it is too far," Thomas reported, his own discomfort at the vampire's warnings apparent in his tone. "He says there is no water in this season, and little game, and that we would all perish on such a journey."

Here Selous spoke up. "I have heard similar cautions many dozens of time, Miss Monot. An African is not unlike any of us in this. He will make the prospects of an action appear dire or rewarding in proportion to his own desire or disinclination for the matter at hand to proceed."

I nodded, understanding, for had not I often employed animadversion concerning the dullness of an upcoming social event simply to cater to my own lethargy?

"We are a small group, and have no oxen to slow us," I reminded Thomas and thus Shaka, "and our needs for water will be less than those of a large trading party. We will tarry here long enough to fashion additional containers out of hide, and we will carry all the water and meat we are capable of transporting. But we *will* make this journey, we *will* find these people, and we *will* bend them to our cause."

It was apparently clear to both my translator and the vampire that my tone would brook no further argument. The former nodded his understanding and the latter appeared happy enough to leave our company and scamper back to his own little fire beyond the borders of our encampment.

Thus it was that some few days later, with Melissa heavily packed, and Thomas, Robert, Michael and even my Coilcycle burdened with skins of water and bundles of dried meat, we broke our little camp and, following Shaka's lead, set off in the cool of the evening on the next leg of our adventure. If I was concerned for myself, given that the food and water we carried would do nothing to sustain me, and considering the African vampire's predictions of a paucity of game, such worries were far overshadowed by my renewed enthusiasm and my determination to accomplish the mission the Lady of the City had charged me with, and thus to make my fortune. As a child on a sled teeters on the edge of a precipice before abandoning herself to cruel gravity, I felt myself on the cusp of a rush of events that would soon sweep me forward, to either success or destruction.

Chapter 15

CHAPTER 15

Following Shaka's lead—A changing countryside— Water becoming scarce—New animals encountered— Trouble with a rhinoceros—Melissa in danger—Tracking the villain—A poor shot—Saved by Selous—Emotions aroused by danger—Seeking privacy in the African night —A consummation devoutly to be wished—Guilt and satisfaction.

If Shaka were hesitant to take us to the creatures he termed "less than," it seems he was even more unwilling to incur my displeasure, as he stepped out smartly and led us on an unwavering course. For several days the country continued unchanged, and we had access to good water and game enough to avoid depleting the stores we carried. Among the animals we encountered was a large wild pig appropriately called wart-hog, which I brought down with a neat shot in the manner earlier described. A city girl, without any experience with domestic swine, I was surprised to find that the blood of this most ungainly of creatures tasted not unlike that of a human, and thus was at least slightly pleasing as well as refreshing.

As we continued onward, however, the nature of the terrain gradually changed, with trees and brush giving way to grasslands. The pasture on these was knee-high, yellow, and brittle dry where it stood; for great swaths of it had been

75

burnt off, whether through an accident of nature or some form of primitive agriculture or husbandry I could not say.

Here water would be scarce until the commencement of the rains brought the land to life again, and many of the pools to which Shaka lead us unerringly were either dry or so alkaline and befouled by animals as to be unpalatable. The diversity of game that we had encountered earlier was also nowhere to be seen. Here we encountered instead the first I'd seen of the truculent black rhinoceros, while the antelope tribe was represented by the occasional leaping duiker and, when we passed the jumbled, rocky hills of the occasional kopjes, the dainty klipspringers that negotiated such heights with a grace and fearlessness equaling even the white goats of the American Rocky Mountains.

It was with the former of these creatures—immense, bi-horned, and seemingly lacking in both acute eyesight and patience—that our little group had an encounter that, given its aftermath, is perhaps worth recounting.

We had established a camp near a slightly less than odious waterhole and, with full darkness upon us and confounding the vision of most of my companions, had settled there for the evening. I was in my tent attending to the recordings that allow this narrative, the Great Hunter was, I think, stealing a moment of sleep, and the boys were seated around the guttering campfire exchanging stories before giving in to slumber themselves.

It was Shaka, ever at the periphery of our assembly, who first gave the alarm, and shortly thereafter I heard the distinctive steam-engine huffing and whisper of grasses indicating that a large animal was approaching our camp at great speed. Though I had never been charged by one before, I immediately identified our adversary as a rhinoceros, for if ever a sound painted the picture of its maker, this one did.

Shouting at Thomas to build up the fire, I was out of my tent in an instant, my suddenly insubstantial-feeling Gibbs clutched firmly in my hands. My admonition came too late, however, for, trampling right through the glowing remnants of the coals, the monster made directly for Melissa. Not a little surprised by the attack, I think, my horse managed to sidestep the upward hook of the creature's horned snout, which punctured one of our precious water skins and carried off, as well, a bundle of dried kudu meat.

Selous was by my side now, his own little Gibbs unshouldered and shouting to Thomas and Michael to bring up the larger double barreled Express rifles. Once it was determined that we all had escaped without physical injury, the Hunter announced that we could not let this attack go unpunished, as the loss of the bundle of meat might mean the failure of our entire enterprise. Taking one of the 500-caliber double rifles and a handful of the remaining cigar-sized cartridges himself, and bidding me abandon my Gibbs for its mate, he instructed our crew to toss enough logs onto the remains of the fire to provide us with a beacon for our return and, nodding to me with an almost boyish smile of excitement, set off in pursuit of the rhinoceros.

Though it was indeed dark, there was enough of a moon to cast a poor light over the country, and even without the benefit of my own night vision the trail of the careening beast must have been easy to discern. It seemed to have never entertained a thought of circling back on our camp to attempt more damage, but only continued in the direction determined by its attack, going at a great pace for almost half a mile before, whatever insult it had imagined fleeing from its poor brain, it settled down to a more restrained pace and soon apparently returned to feeding as if nothing had happened.

Thus it was that the Great Hunter and I discovered our quarry, moving slowly along and oblivious to our pursuit, with the torn rag of our water sack and the bundle of meat still flopping over its little pig-eyes with every step.

Selous stepped close, and I was not surprised by the little thrill that his nearness occasioned me. Keeping an eye on the beast and, I noticed, careful to nowhere touch me no matter how near he leaned, he whispered. "Would you like to do the honors, Miss Monot? You are clearly a proficient nimrod, and might benefit from the experience of firing the larger rifle."

I nodded silently, and, with Selous backing me up, tried to draw a bead on the creature before us. The double rifle, though doubtless an elegant device of fine manufacture, had little of the lithe grace of my Gibbs, and although its weight was of course nothing to me, I struggled a bit to keep the front bead locked in the deep "V" of the rear sight and both of them on the shoulder of the rhinoceros.

I had only just done so to my satisfaction when a nightjar, which had, apparently, lay huddled upon the sand nearby for some time before its feathered courage broke, burst into raucous flight at my very feet. Startled, I pulled the trigger unintentionally and, my aim broken by the bird's explosive flush, struck the poor beast too high.

Upon feeling the bullet, the monster pivoted more rapidly than any show horse and, from less than fifty yards away, thundered toward us with evil intent. Still confident in my abilities, I was already centering the bead sight upon a point between the animal's piggish eyes with the intent of loosing my second barrel when Selous stepped between me and the charging rhinoceros and, bringing his own rifle to his shoulder in what appeared to be a single unbroken motion, fired a shot that dropped the beast immediately, though so close to us that the moonlit dust raised by its fall sifted gently onto our shoes.

Emotions are wont to flare with the sudden passing of danger, and I can assure you that ours did little to contradict this rule. I was, at least initially, angry at the Hunter's apparent presumption that I, a Modern Woman, had been in need of masculine intervention and rescue. In that mood I rounded on him, and prepared to strongly remonstrate. You can imagine my surprise, then, when, dropping his rifle to the grass, he seized me by the shoulders and kissed me full on the mouth.

Unanticipated or no, I returned that kiss. Selous clutched me close, and I was immediately aware of his arousal. The poor man had, I surmised, been building to this state ever since I had caressed him intimately during our last dalliance. His hands were on me, seeking any access to the skin beneath my clothing, and I found this attention altogether pleasing but I feared that the sound of our gunshots would call our fellows to us despite the stygian darkness, and I had no wish to be discovered in *flagrant delecte*. Thus I grabbed my ardent squire's hands (which were fair trembling with eagerness) and, kissing him prettily on the lips, urged him to collect his rifle and follow me further into the veldt where we might continue our tryst without fear of discovery.

The African night is inky and deep, though this presented no great impediment to my augmented vision. It is also, however, the province of the great cats, who rejoice in the cover of darkness, which greatly facilitates their hunting. My companion and I had little thought for such dangers, however, as we at length arrived at a small green hill some distance from the fallen rhinoceros.

Here I stopped and, removing my short riding cape (which I had earlier donned for, no matter the heat of the day, the nights in this part of the country were brisk), I spread its inadequate blanket upon the cushion of grass.

Ours were not circumstances conducive to complete disrobing, so I merely loosened and lowered my garments above to free my breasts (and oh, dear ladies, is there not in truth a little frisson of thrill whenever we bare our bosoms to the night sky?). Then, stepping free of my bloomers and lifting my skirt up over my hips, I reclined on the makeshift blanket and raised my arms to my erstwhile champion.

He however, though ever so eager just moments ago, seems transfixed by the sight of so much white skin. Leaning forward, I unlaced his breeches, immediately noting that his interest had in no way slackened, and then, lifting my knees, lay back and beckoned him again.

With a cry he fell forward, mouth to my breast and clumsily trying to find his entry below. I lifted my hips to him and, with one hand, guided the head of his cock to its goal, upon which, with a groan, he plunged it fully into me. I confess I cried out as well, as he was nicely made and it had been some time since I was so entered. My outburst only added to his passion, and he moved atop my belly roughly and with increasing fervor until, all too soon, he ground his hips tight against me and I felt the scalding heat of his ejaculation within the cool depths of my flesh.

When the spasms had quite passed, he rolled off me, muttering apologies. I however, leaned over him and, with a flurry of kisses, informed him that his haste was his only sin, and that I intended to allow him to absolve himself of it thoroughly. With that I set about restoring his ardor with the attention of my hands and mouth (for I was feeling altogether aroused and thus deliciously bawdy). When he was quite ready, I straddled him and, with deliberate intent, impaled myself with teasing slowness. His eyes were wide with wonder as I proceeded to rock myself forward and up before taking him in again, each time milking the length of him with my inner muscles as I rose and loosening them to engulf him as I settled.

By paying careful attention to his degree of arousal, and alternately slowing and speeding my pace (at times stopping altogether and pinning him there as he tried in vain to continue lifting himself against me), I was able to prolong the bout nicely and, when I felt ready to surrender to my own pleasure, rode him quickly to another hot release.

The Great Hunter fair peppered me with apologies as we straightened our garments, but I refused these one and all, telling him that there were few enough pleasures in this world, and that I was determined not to begrudge myself this, one of the sweetest among them. Thus with the matter apparently settled, though I knew he still wrestled with unspoken guilt, we made our way back to the site of the shooting, only to discover that my caution had been unnecessary, and we had not been followed. (Though I assure you that, had we not already had an ample supply of meat in camp, no terror could have kept our little safari from the promise of fresh fat.)

Chapter 16

Water increasingly scarce—No longer pretend interest in tea—A borehole at last—Thomas begs we abandon our mission—I set out in search of water—An elephant too close—A desperate shot—The little Gibbs works wonders—Water from the titan's stomach—Our trek saved.

Once the rhinoceros had been butchered, and its fat rendered and meat made ready for travel, we once again took to the trail on the heels of a decidedly more reluctant Shaka. As the days passed, what had once been an unbroken sea of grasslands or a burnt-off desolation took on a poorer appearance still, with even the tufts of brittle yellow-baked grasses becoming rarer, and the expanses of sand between these ever greater. I soon decided that there had been some truth to our guide's warnings, as water became increasingly scarce, and we were more than once forced to turn to the reserves that we carried for this (to everyone but me and Shaka) mainstay of life itself.

With our shortages in mind, and realizing that since my nature was now known to all there was no advantage to be earned by subterfuge, I abandoned my pretend interest in tea, the better to assure water supplies remained for the Hunter and our crew, and for poor Melissa who was often so dry that she showed no interest in what food was available to her. Selous insisted upon my feeding before weakness overcame me, though these communions were perfunctory, since to engage in anything more frivolous would only deplete his energies further. Shaka ranged out from our camp in the evenings, and though I know he found small lives enough to keep him ambulatory, even he rapidly lost condition as the landscape grew ever more foreboding.

Thus you can imagine our relief when, some nights hence, the African vampire lead us to a borehole. Here generations of natives had dug ever further after the retreating water. It was quite eight feet deep and small in diameter, but by lowering a tin cup on a string we were able to bring up a swallow of the precious liquid at a time, and eventually provided some ease to the human members of our party, and even enough for my brave horse to allow her to listlessly chew on the sparse, tinder-dry grasses.

That evening Thomas approached me, with a hangdog expression, and begged me to give up our quest. To venture further into the wastes without a clear prospect for water would be certain death, he sobbed, his distress clearly quite genuine. If we would but tarry here, he insisted, we could gradually acquire enough fitness to enable us to retrace our tracks to safety.

I was loath to give up my mission, and yet the sincerity of Thomas's appeal told on me, as did the fact that even Selous here said nothing to contradict him. Giving the matter some thought, I announced that they should indeed stay put and husband their resources, but that I would (on my Coilcycle, for Melissa was in no condition to carry more than the burden we had already charged her with) ride ahead in one final effort to find a way out of our dire predicament.

Once the matter was settled in my mind, I would brook no argument and, slipping my Gibbs into the Cycle's scabbard, I rolled silently off into the thickening evening.

Though I had put on a determined front, when the lights of the campfires had faded behind me I was forced to admit that my situation was quite serious. Despite the Great Hunter's generosity, I was nothing like at my full strength, and no matter how acute my senses, there was no guarantee that I would come upon water before what energy I had failed me.

In this gloomy state of mind I wheeled along for some time. It was likely due to my preoccupation, as well as the relative silence of my mechanical steed, that I suddenly found myself only feet away from a bull elephant which, as it had been standing motionless, perhaps trying to determine my nature, I had mistaken for one of the many huge termite mounds that dotted the ground over which I had been travelling.

Knowing I was far too close to the great beast, I grabbed at my brakes, causing the Cycle's mainspring to squeal loudly against this sudden constriction. At the noise the creature turned and I was only able to drag my front wheel around and race off at a right angle before it, with great ears out and a deafening trumpet, set off after me.

The thick sand so dragged at my wheels that I had but half my usual speed, and for a moment I was only able to stay ahead of the monster by constantly cutting new angles, thus denying him direct access to my scent. This was heavy work, though, and it took its toll upon my control of the Cycle, to the point that I cut one such turn too sharply and the lugged wheels slid out from under me. The elephant was close on my heels when this happened and, abandoning my mount to what I thought was its certain destruction, I rolled from it and sprinted for the cover of the nearest termite mound.

From that shelter, I was surprised to see the creature approach my cycle gingerly, and, touching it with its great trunk, examine it with curiosity but no apparent malicious intent. Remembering that Selous had once spoken of the reserves of potable water often found in the stomachs of these African monarchs, and knowing that I was approaching the limits of my endurance, I then decided to attempt to bring the immense creature to bag.

My little .360 Gibbs was perhaps ill suited to this task, but I took heart in the knowledge that Selous had himself brought down elephants with his rifle, which was, while of a larger caliber than mine, still widely believed to be inadequate for the biggest game. Sorting through the cartridges in my pouch and selecting a solid tipped round with which to replace the expanding bullet already chambered, I determined to salute my quarry and to stake the entire success of our enterprise upon this action.

Creeping on my hands and knees to some twenty yards from where the elephant still puzzled over my abandoned mount, I made ready to fire for a spot behind his shoulder, with the aim of piercing both his lungs, when I felt the wind shift to my back, blowing my scent directly toward the great beast.

In the moments that followed I quickly realized that, in his earlier pursuit, the elephant had merely been hunting for me, and not actually charging. When doing so he had often spread his great ears and lifted his trunk in the air, as elephants in penny dreadful illustrations are shown to do when "attacking." With me clearly in sight and scent, though, the creature came at a great pace, silent and with its ears back and trunk curled over its chest.

Time seemed to slow, as it often does in moments of crisis, and though only seconds passed, I recalled Selous' description of the elephant's brain (for no other shot would stop him quickly enough to prevent my demise) as being no bigger than a loaf of bread; and remembered the drawings he had made in the sand to educate me on the position of that organ. All that information passed through my mind in the time it took to raise my little rifle and, drawing a bead on the point which I believed would allow my hardened bullet to find the soft target behind its wall of bone, I fired.

I was almost shocked when the mighty creature collapsed to the shot, dropping to his front knees and, after sliding some distance forward, pushing a wave of sand before it, balancing there. Its great tusked head rocked back and forth slightly with momentum, though all conscious life had already fled. Taking my knife, I quickly sliced open one of the veins that spider-webbed a fanned ear, and ate there to repletion while the great heart stumbled and stopped, after which I returned with due haste to bring my safari forward.

We found fully ten gallons of water in the creature's stomach, clear and, though warm, not foul in flavor (or so I was told). More important still, Selous assured me that the elephant must have recently drunk to be carrying so much. Backtracking its trail, we discovered a small pool hidden beneath an overhang of rock. Thus with a renewed supply of water and more meat than we could carry (though I assure you that every bit of fat was consumed before we left the carcass), the sword of doom was at least temporarily removed from above us.

For several days after leaving this oasis we continued through an unchanging wasteland, poor in water, forage, and game. It was a time of suffering for all members of our little party, but the trials we endured were all of a kind, and not significantly different from the events already described, so I will not burden the reader with an extended narrative. Suffice to say we oft made do with water that was little more than mud, once again resorting to straining it through blankets, and that Selous' generosity kept me on my feet, while Shaka ranged across the desert as we travelled and found enough small creatures to sustain himself (though he increasingly eyed Melissa hungrily, and was surely the author of many a nightmare suffered by my crew).

Eventually, however, the nature of the lands around us began to vary. The rare tufts of sunburnt grass gave way to brush-land, and once again the stately acacia trees added the lace of their limbs to the sunset sky. As the terrain changed, so did the numbers and variety of game animals increase, indicating a more reliable supply of water. In fact, on our second day of travel through this new country, we came upon a small river, delightfully clear and, in its slower reaches, even bedecked in water lilies, upon which the mood of our little party improved markedly.

Chapter 17

Rest and respite by a water hole--Fresh rations for the camp—Shaka sets some ground rules—A reluctant compromise—A telltale footprint—Tracking the "less thans"—Into a Bushman vampire camp—Crudeness of shelters—Like fishing with poor bait—The creatures appear—Crudeness of their weapons—Appearance of the Elder—Communication finally established—I prove my mettle over a strange dinner—A singular success.

We determined to tarry for a day at this site; to refresh ourselves, wash the stain of hard miles from our clothing, and lay our plans for the next stage of our journey. Selous and I also took the opportunity to obtain some fresh rations, for we had been unable to carry much of the elephant earlier killed, and the realities of travel had reduced our menu to the shade-dried meat known as biltong for much of the adventure thus far. We were fortunate to encounter a small herd of elands not too distant from our camp, one of which the Hunter dropped without drama or fanfare, securing fat and flesh for our camp and a sup for me which, though inferior to that which he could have offered, allowed him the opportunity to regain his strength without the added burden of seeing to my own needs simultaneously.

We would, Shaka assured us, arrive within the territory of the vampires we sought within a day's travel should we not encounter unanticipated delays. Our guide further advised us that, upon reaching that goal, we had best establish a camp from which a small party, consisting of only him and me, could sally forward in an attempt to make contact with these mysterious creatures. Selous of course objected to this plan, but Shaka insisted that the "less-thans" would not allow themselves to be seen by a larger group.

"They *fear*, they will *hide*," he insisted through Thomas' translation; but upon being reminded that I could not understand his language, nor certainly that of the people we sought, he assented to have our translator travel with us, to be left behind within hailing range while Shaka and I moved into the vampire's camp proper and attempted to belay their fears with our actions alone, after which Thomas could be called forward and more complex communications commence.

This compromise was eventually, albeit reluctantly on the part of the Hunter, accepted by all. So, refreshed and energized by this refinement of our strategy, we set off. The country was now quite lovely, with grasslands broken by little islands of brush and occasional stands of graceful trees, giving the land something of the appearance of a tame English deer park. It was in no way so benign, or course, as were reminded one late afternoon when, passing through a grassy meadow, we startled a small group of lions that had apparently been slumbering through the decline of the day.

The young animals (so Selous afterwards assured us they had been) got up quite under our feet, more startling than any flushing covey of British grouse. Fortunately, they decided to take to their heels rather than contest with us, and we suffered little more than a moment's fright and a renewed edge to the caution that the gentle seeming landscape had perhaps inappropriately dulled.

Coming upon a sand river that meandered in an appropriate direction, mostly dry save for a thin trickle of clear water that still wound its way through the wide flood-season bed, we at once took advantage of this natural highway. Selous was just calling to my attention a trio of magnificent sable antelope bulls that were cautiously watching our progress from a patch of brush some one hundred yards to our left, when Shaka, who had as ever been walking to the fore of our party, came to a halt as sudden as a bird dog going on point, and waved frantically for the Hunter and me to come forward.

This we did, and found before him, in a patch of sand still darkened by the water that had since fled beneath it, a single footprint. It was quite perfect in its distinctness, but was of a size that might have been made by a child of five or six. With Robert's arrival, we asked our guide the significance of this spoor, and he assured us the track had been made by one of the "less thans," and furthermore that the foot that had left this tantalizing mark had belonged to a fully grown adult male.

Shaka evinced great excitement, and not a little nervousness, at this discovery. Speaking through our translator, he insisted that it was imperative that we now put our previously agreed upon plan into action. Therefore we established a camp in the brush some distance from the creek bed and, when this was set up and skermed with a thorn-bush hedge to Selous' satisfaction, Robert, our guide, and I set off on our own.

I of course continued on my Coilcycle, my Gibbs in its scabbard, my pepper-box pistol in a pocket, and an ammunition bag over my shoulder. Our translator carried one of the double .500 Express rifles, and I must note seemed to take precious little comfort from the presence of that weapon. Other than this we bore only water and food for Thomas, and a small sack of what poor trading gifts had survived the earlier attack of the Matabele and the avarice of the African vampire queen.

Though I rode my brakes to slow my speed, the cycle still covered ground far faster than my companions on foot, so I found myself riding back and forth in front of them, my trail undulating like Christmas ribbon candy. This course gave me ample opportunity to study the ground in front of us, and I soon began to notice more and more of the diminutive footprints. Shaka clearly saw them as well, as evidenced by his ever growing nervousness. Finally he came to a stop and addressed an urgent rattle of syllables to Thomas.

"He says I must stop here," my major domo translated. "He says the creatures are quite near at hand." Thomas was clearly unnerved, his fine black skin taking on a sickly grey hue. Looking about, I spotted a great tree, the shade of which would serve to hide him, and which was surrounded by a large clearing, allowing him a substantial field of view (and a field of fire as well, though I of course hoped it would not come to that).

Stepping off my Coilcycle and resting it upon the kick stand, I indicated this sanctuary with a wave of my arm.

"It will be as we planned then, Robert." I said. "You remain there, and keep your rifle handy. But do not shoot unless you must, as the success of our endeavor depends upon our earning the trust of these people. Wait for our call, and when you hear it, come forward showing signs of neither fear nor threat."

He obeyed this command wordlessly, though every line of his body screamed that he would find my final admonition difficult to follow at best. Then nodding to Shaka, whose language remained a mystery to me, I waved him forward, and together we entered the thickening brush.

The path we travelled soon became quite compact, as if the weight of countless little feet had, over time, compressed and defined it. Eventually it gave way to a small clearing, and here Shaka stopped, pointing before him as if there were something he would have me see. At first I could discern nothing, and then, like those novelty drawings that first appear to be one thing and suddenly reveal themselves to be quite another, the scene before me came into focus.

There were no constructed shelters, but beneath the overhanging branches of the thickest of the bushes dried grass had been piled into poor beds, and I saw the edges of several little fire rings, doused and hastily covered with twig and weed. It was a village, though crude in the extreme, and more akin to something one would expect from a colony of apes than sentient beings. I confess to indulging in a moment of concern at the sheer otherness of it, but I quickly marshaled my nerves.

Our quarry had not been ignorant of our coming, and even Shaka and I alone had seemed threat enough to cause them to flee. Using hand gestures in place of language, I tried to convey to my guide that I wished him to retreat. When he had done so I, carrying the small sack of trinkets we had been able to salvage, walked into the center of the clearing and sat down.

Patience comes easier to those of us not enslaved by time, and yet I had begun to doubt the wisdom of this course of action when, some two hours later, I finally espied a small face peering at me from the surrounding bush. I did not show my teeth, thinking it likely that the little creatures had long since determined that Shaka and I shared their nature, and that if we had been less than what we were we would in all likelihood already be dead.

Instead, moving slowly so as not to startle, I fished into the bag of gifts and lifted out a poorly made rhinestone necklace. This I dangled from my hand, letting it catch the light of the rising moon, and then placed upon the ground before me.

The face disappeared, and some minutes later revealed itself in another location. At this time I was able to make sure that my guest was, as I had surmised, a woman, for she wore no clothing of any sort and, though diminutive in the extreme, was fully and neatly formed. She vanished again as I dropped the trinket, only to reappear somewhat closer to where I sat. I made no movement, following her only with my eyes, until curiosity got the better of her fear and she dashed forward, picked up the necklace, and fled back into the bush as if the devil himself pursued her.

I made no move to follow, but, reaching into the bag again, retrieved a tiara of pot metal and paste stones, and placed this on the grass where the previous trinket had been. Again I waited, aware that the calls of the night birds were loudly announcing their ascendance over their cousins of the day. This time my vigil was not so lengthy, though, as in less than half an hour another woman appeared, looking somewhat older than the first, and repeated the former's peek-a-boo approach before also darting in to capture the prize and then scrambling away.

When this wordless pantomime had been repeated three more times, in every case the participant being a different woman, I stood and walked off, turning my back to the occupied bushes with the appearance of nonchalance. I detected no effort to follow and so, when I judged myself far enough from the camp, called out for Shaka and Thomas to come forward, assuming that, though the former would not understand my meaning, the sound of my voice alone would serve as a summons.

This it did, and soon they had both joined me, Shaka expressing great caution in his every step and my translator clutching his Express rifle as if it were a lifeline. I bade them follow me into the clearing and there we sat, shoulder to shoulder in triangular formation in order to command all fields of view, with my eyes on the bushes that had so recently disgorged some representatives of the people we sought.

Again I rummaged through the bag of trifles, this time pulling forth a box of safety matches, as I remembered the impact these had had on the vampire queen. One of those I lit, holding it up like a tiny torch against the night sky and then, blowing it out, set the box on the spot from which my earlier offerings had been taken.

I could feel poor Thomas shivering against my shoulder, but I did not dare speak any words of comfort, instinct telling me that silence would best advance our endeavor. This is not to say that the setting was in any way quiet; on the contrary the night birds, now joined by a rising chorus of insects, set up an absolute din, but as even the music of the surf is soon ignored by those so fortunate as to live adjacent to it, this background noise in short order came to seem merely another face of silence.

Presently a rustling in the brush announced movement within, and I gave the knees of both of my companions a quick squeeze to reassure them. A moment later the source of these sounds was revealed, as two small men stepped from the bush, one on either side of our party, with miniature bows drawn and tiny arrows trained upon us.

These weapons were quite peculiar. Being both small and crudely made, they looked like nothing but the toys an American child might fashion from a hickory stick in order to play at wild Indians. It was clear to me that such small catapults alone would be useless against anything but the smallest of lizards and rodents, so I surmised that the arrows (which seemed to have no heads attached, being only whittled to a point on the striking end and, by the look of it, hardened in a fire) were augmented by some sort of poison. This I later discovered to be the case.

The two warriors (for though lacking stature, this is indeed what they were) continued to cover us with their bows, while we, with my cautionary hands adding what comfort they could to my companions, sat all motionless. Long minutes trickled slowly by as we held this little tableau, but eventually the brush immediately in front of me parted to disclose an extraordinary creature.

The woman so revealed appeared to be even smaller than her compatriots, and I presumed she had been aged when she was made, and perhaps even selected for the gift on the basis of her mortal wisdom (for so is it sometimes done even by our kind in the enlightened world; we are not, in fact, all of us eternally young and beautiful). Her appearance was wizened and, where the others of her clan that we had so far seen wore nothing but the skin that they were born with, she sported a sort of skirt of the tails of small animals and strips of hide, which hung quite to the ground and indeed trailed along it. Her right hand, delicate as a child's, was warped into a twisted claw from some long ago catastrophe.

After studying us for some time she spoke, a burst of hard vowels punctuated by clicks and pops of the tongue against the roof of the mouth. I looked at Thomas and was distressed to see no more comprehension in his wide eyed face that I myself enjoyed. So, gazing at the strange apparition all the while, I spoke in a carefully calm tone of voice for my translator's instruction.

"Try what languages you have, Thomas. Tell her we have no ill intent. Tell her we come to treat and with gifts to offer." This he did, mastering the quaver in his voice quite manfully.

I watched the creature's eyes as my translator tried his catalog of languages, and finally thought I perceived a flicker of recognition on the crone's wrinkled face.

"That one, Thomas," I said, calmly and reasonably, as if placing an order in a shop, "repeat the message again in that tongue." He did, in what I was later to learn was his own language, that of the MaShona, and after some moments the woman replied, the words apparently difficult for her to form, and awkwardly shaped.

"She says that Shaka is of their enemies, and that the more-thans of every tribe fear her people and try to kill them when they can. She asks why you bring a lamb, by this she means me, Miss, into a village of leopards." My good man somehow kept his voice calm as he said this, though his knee beneath my hand was fair rattling against the ground. I should mention here that, with this exchange, I began to understand that the phrases "less than" and "more than" referred to physical stature rather than any perceived cultural inferiority or superiority.

"Tell her that Shaka has left his people to join us, and that I represent a mighty tribe of our kind far away. Tell her that I do not travel with sheep but only lions, be they warm or cold. Tell her that her enemies can be mine, and that we seek to end the terror that Lobengula's Impis have brought to all in this land." Here I knew I had scored a telling point, for her strange yellow eyes quite blazed at the name of the Savage King. After a moment she replied, and Thomas continued to translate.

"She says she sees you for what you are, Miss, and admits that perhaps you do not speak falsely. But she claims that the Impis cannot reach her people here, and that any stray Matabele who wanders this brush-land becomes not conqueror but the occasion for a feast." Through all this I attempted to read her eyes, while my tinted lenses limited her access to my own. It was clear that she was both proud and suspicious, so I determined to throw the dice and show her that I was neither intimidated nor dissuaded.

"Tell her I say that Lobengula's armies don't reach her here only because she has already run before them. Tell her that if the Matabele are not contained there will soon be nowhere to run. If she will ally her people with me, the Terrible King will be brought down and she will again be free to hunt in richer lands." At this Thomas turned his eyes to me, wordlessly pleading that I send a more conciliatory message. I, however, only added the weight of command to my speech (for her benefit as much as his) and said, "Tell her!"

Brought up short by my tone (for I had for the most part been gentle of voice when speaking to my people), Thomas repeated the message with his own little show of bravado. Out of the corners of my eyes I saw the bowmen bring their drawn strings to their cheeks, but I kept my focus solely upon the old woman before me.

At first her dried-apple face gave little away, but after a moment she smiled (though it was a disconcerting smile, given that, as had been the case with Shaka's people, her feeding teeth were in a state of permanent erection). She followed this grin with a short burst of speech, at which I noticed the warriors relaxing their weapons.

Thomas, too, appeared to sigh with relief before he conveyed her message.

"She says that she is not yet convinced that you are a lion, miss, but she sees that neither are you like an eland cow to be driven along in order to slaughter it where one wishes. She asks that you show her what gifts you bring to prove your friendship."

At this I returned her smile, and let my own teeth slide briefly out of my gums. My erstwhile host was unable to conceal her surprise at this display, from which I surmised that her people were without this means of disguise that had so facilitated my kin's ability to move among the warm blooded of our civilized world.

Taking up the box of matches, I again lit one and blew it out, and doing so pushed the container toward her. Searching in the sack, I pulled forth also a small folding knife, demonstrating its mechanism, another rhinestone necklace, and a bandana in red and white paisley pattern. I at first feared the inadequacy of these poor offerings, but was rewarded with a look of pure avarice on her wizened features, and so added the last to the pile with confidence.

The woman stepped forward and collected my offerings, immediately adding the little scarf (for it seemed that this had most attracted her interest) to the tails and strips of hide that made up her only article of clothing. The necklace joined it there, taking pride of place in the front and center of her garment. She made no effort to manipulate either the folding knife or the matches, my little demonstration apparently enough to assure her that these would present no challenges to her clever little hands, wounded though one might be.

Here she seated herself before me and with a few words in her own tongue sent her two bowmen off into the brush. Soon the unmistakable sound of a heavy burden being drug across the ground reached us, and the warriors reappeared, their weapons slung over their necks by the strings, dragging a trussed-up man whose size and garments identified him as Matabele.

Bound hand and foot, this captive also appeared to be drugged to insensibility, I presumed by the effects of the poisoned arrows. The woman had him dragged to a position alongside us, and then addressed me in the MaShona tongue. I feared I guessed the import of this development, but nonetheless turned to Thomas for confirmation.

"She says this is her gift to you, miss, and asks that you cement your friendship with her by joining her in eating of the blood of your mutual enemy." Thomas somehow kept his voice calm while delivering this message, but I could see that the effort cost him dearly, and that tears now streaked the dust upon is cheeks.

I examined the captive more carefully, thinking that in so doing I might buy myself additional time to consider my options. Upon closer study, it became apparent to me that he had been fed upon before, and that an advanced state of exsanguination, rather than arrow-borne poisons, might account for his senseless state. Though Thomas knew quite well what I was, he had yet to see me feed on human blood, and I knew not how such a spectacle might impact him. On the other hand, although I believed that I might still win the allegiance of these people if I spurned the offering, I also knew that such an insult would delay the process, and that time was not our friend.

These considerations sped through my mind in fewer seconds than it takes to write them. Deciding that fate rewards the bold, I again unsheathed my teeth and, with a smile for my host, leaned forward and sank them into the neck of the bound man, tasting human blood for the first time in far too long. In truth it was delicious, and though I could detect a faint taint that I made sure was, indeed, the lingering poison from the little arrows, I knew as soon as it hit my tongue that this toxin was no threat to me. It was only with an effort of will that I stopped myself before I had drained him quite completely, and sat up, offering, with a wave of my hand, the final dainties to my hostess.

While I fed Shaka had not taken his eyes from me, and trembled with desire like a fly-worried horse. The little woman had of course noticed this and, in a gesture that I thought exceedingly magnanimous, offered the dregs of this cup of life to him with a nod of her head. He did not need a second invitation, and fell upon the captive greedily. Soon it became clear that this victim lived no more. I found it curious, in fact (as I often had in the past), that, though the man was in both states immobile, the passage to death was so obvious to the eye and abrupt.

With our sup finished, the tiny vampire (whose name I came to learn was "Xam," with the "x" pronounced as our "k," and preceded by a click of the tongue on the roof of the mouth) spoke again. I was pleased to see that, despite the horrors he had seen me perform, Thomas had regained some of his poise (for the human mind can, it seems, adjust itself to anything in time). He translated as she spoke, indicating that we had much to discuss, and that she would be pleased if we would linger in her village, resting in the heat of the coming day, and parlay with her again.

To this I acceded, explaining only that there were several more in our party whom we had left behind for fear of disturbing her and her people, apparently the act of my feeding upon her human gift had quite driven all suspicion from her mind, for she only nodded absently at this information and bade me make haste and bring them forward that we might establish a campsite before sunrise. This I did and, leaving Thomas and Shaka behind, had soon walked to my Coilcycle and, in a very short time, rejoined Selous and the others with news of what I could only think had been my singular success.

Chapter 18

Establish a camp near the Bushman village—The structure of their society—Hatred for the Matabele—I offer an alliance—Selous doubts the efficacy of our new allies—A plan to treat with the African King—Uncertainly among my followers—Xam demands to look into my heart.

Since Xam's village was quite devoid of huts (or really anything a civilized person might term a shelter), we established our own camp at a slight distance and surrounded it, as usual, with a skerm of tightly woven thorn bush, more as protection against lions and other marauding beasts than because of any suspicion as to the motives of the miniature vampires, whom I believed had been quite won over.

Indeed so it developed upon the following evening. Again I met with Xam, and again offered her some little tokens to open our negotiations. She, it seems, knew that I would have no need to feed again so soon, and so I was spared the delicious guilt of partaking of another of her gifts.

I learned, as I had assumed, that theirs was indeed a matriarchal society, and that she was its titular head, though more group-mother than queen. Their manner of governing was unusual in the extreme, as it appears that each assumed responsibility for the good of his or her neighbors, to the point that captives (such as the one I had enjoyed) were returned to the village and shared among the inhabitants, with the most needy receiving priority of place. In this way, it reminded me of the false vine of Marxism that has recently threatened to take root in poor Europe,

They had, indeed, fled from richer pastures to escape the depredations of the Matabele, but counted also the MaShona, and indeed Shaka's people as well, among their oppressors. And the move had not been without sacrifice. In fact, the root of the hatred with which they had been regarded by their former neighbors lay in the regular levy, to be paid in human life, which Xam's people had collected from those who lived around them. Since being driven off, they found food much more difficult to come by, and the old woman confessed that there was dissatisfaction among her followers.

This was my moment. I leapt forth into a narration of the power of the English, and of their shared desire to see Lobengula and his Impis punished for the terror they had brought to these lands. With Robert's help, for he had quite resigned himself to the horrors of the world he now inhabited, I assured her that, with her people's aid, this noble mission could not fail, and they would then be free to, without fear, return to their ancestral home. Most telling of all, perhaps, I promised them sole access to the blood of their enemies, both wounded and captured.

"Your people will feast, Xam, so grandly that your name will be told in tales that will live on to thrill those yet unmade, and be remembered as a time when the smallest of women strode largest across the stage of the world."

With this stirring admonition I immediately saw that I had won her over, and before the hour was gone she had gathered her village to her, and echoing my words in her own strange tongue, soon had them whipped to a cheering frenzy, beating the hard earth with their little feet and waving their bows above their heads in a manner quite demonic. I had, it seemed, acquired my army.

Selous, however, was not so certain. In the days that followed, while Xam's people made ready to march with us, the Great Hunter was always about. It seems that he, alone among the warm blooded members of my party, harbored no fear of the diminutive vampires, even pitching in to help them tie up bundles and organize their few worldly goods for efficient transport. One evening, upon returning to our campfire from these duties, he drew me aside.

"I fear they are too small, Miss Monot," he began. I was on the verge of protesting that he might use my given name, considering how matters stood between us, but his serious expression convinced me that now was not the time for flirtation.

"Not in size," he went on, "but in number. I have been through quite the entire camp, and, man and woman, there are not above three dozen people here. Even if they were giants, it would not be enough to turn the tide against Lobengula's thousands."

I made ready to protest, to remind the Hunter of the psychological effect Shaka's attack had inflicted upon the Matabele raiding party, but it seems he anticipated my arguments, for he pressed on.

"They are mysterious creatures, indeed, my dear Paulette," (and here I preened a little bit despite myself, for it was the first time he had used my given name in such a way), "and I am sure even the smallest of them is stronger and faster than a full-sized Matabele warrior. But here I fear that their stature does work against them. An unknowing man will look upon the python with dread because of its size, though there is no danger in it, and disregard the tiny though deadly krait. No, my lady, though Xam's people might be fearless and their arrows toxic, we cannot count upon their engendering the same sort of panic that a monster of Shaka's size inspires."

I confess I wilted at these words, so sudden and precipitous was my fall from joy to despair.

"Then all is lost, my Frederick," I said (giving tit for tat, even in my gloom), "and my mission doomed to failure. I do not think I can bear the disappointment on dear Lady Ellen's face, she who has been so very kind to me."

"We are not quite lost yet," he replied. "We shall play this card and draw another. I have noted with admiration your skills at negotiation with the little people. I move that we send Xam's tiny army, in the company of Shaka and Thomas and the rest, on to the Iron Hill mine, where the British South Africa Company's forces gather to await the battle that all expect to come, giving them leave to pick off the stragglers of any moving Impis they encounter along the way. You and I will beard the lion in his den. I have a long history with Lobengula, and can speak his language tolerable well. I propose we go to his city and that you, as a bonded representative of Cecil Rhodes himself, attempt to cool the fires in his tyrant's breast and bring this war to an end."

I did not answer immediately, in part because I had begun to suspect that preventing the looming hostilities would not please Mr. Rhodes nearly as much as would assuring the triumph of the side upon which he had wagered. Still, however, it is an easy thing to start a war, and the tycoon might at least be grateful for the opportunity to instigate it when circumstances were more to his liking. I also admit to curiosity concerning the Bloodthirsty Monarch, and confess that the chance to see him in his very habitat and at the head of his own savage people would not be an unwelcome opportunity.

Still I demurred. "Might we not be playing into the Monster's hands were we to do so? I may not be of great value as a hostage, but surely Queen and country would be sorely vexed to see the famous Hunter Naturalist taken captive, and might they not even be perhaps moved to give ground in negotiations in order to secure your release?"

Selous was steadfast. "I have walked into the African Tyrant's town before, under omens no less gloomy. The Old Scoundrel might be a demon in mortal form, and hold human life no more sacred than that of the least insect, but he has his honor, and on that card I am willing to wager our safety."

I could argue no more, but though the course of action was decided, there was much to do before implementing it, not the least of which was communicating our decision to the others involved. We wasted no time in doing so, calling together the members of our little party and Xam, representing the force of Bushman vampires, for a pow-wow.

Our announcement was not immediately well received. Thomas, Robert, and Michael did not look with pleasure upon the prospect of being the only warm blooded beings in the midst of a small army of vampires; and Shaka showed great distress at the thought of being separated from me, whom his superstition had charged him to accompany. Selous and I answered these concerns as they arose, meeting them with logic when appropriate and sternness when no other argument would win the day.

Through all this Xam held her council, and it was only when all other concerns had apparently been addressed that she spoke in her own language. Thomas translated, and I was impressed by how quickly his natural abilities have taken him from a complete incomprehension of this alien tongue to its apparent mastery. I recalled Holmes' admonition to not underestimate the capabilities of the primitive mind, and was once more convinced of his wisdom.

"She is worried that, should you successfully treat with Lobengula, her people will be stranded between the hammer of the Impis and the anvil of the white men's forces in Salisbury. She says that though you are her sister, she cannot risk them all on the strength of your word. She says only upon looking onto your heart will her mind be put at ease."

CHAPTER 19

A test I viewed with dread—No choice but to take it—Blood for blood, and secrets for secrets—I look into Xam's memories—Embarrassing secrets revealed—She sees my "heart is white"—New plans laid—Onward to Bulawayo.

I had half anticipated this demand, and I looked upon it with some trepidation. The reassurance Xam sought could only be had through what the kin call a *joining*, wherein two of our kind feed upon each other's wrists simultaneously. It is an act more intimate than any lovemaking, and in the give and take of the hearts thus conjoined all doors are opened and every secret is offered, naked and exposed. I had no fear of her discovering treachery in my motives toward the Bushmen vampires, as I was quite committed to my allegiance with them, but the thought of allowing myself to be otherwise so stripped was fearsome to me, not in the least because the tiny woman was a creature of considerably greater age and power than I.

Certainly the Hunter sensed my concern, and touched my hand to offer comfort, whilst shaking his head to deny the request, but the little Bushman vampire seemed only to find humor in this, and giggled brightly. Shaka, too, understood the risks and stepped forward, offering (through Thomas' translation) to submit to the test in my stead.

Xam frowned upon hearing this offer, and addressed the larger vampire with disdain.

"When one wishes to know how the hunt will proceed," she said, the withering nature of her reply surviving even into through Thomas' intervention, "does one ignore the master and attempt to speak to the dog?   No, it is only through my sister that I might find the comfort that I seek."

My choices were few. Were I to refuse her demand, I would lose what little progress I had made and, should treating with Lobengula fail (as I feared it would), have only my original party to throw into the breach in an effort to stem the coming Matabele floods. On the other hand, I had never participated in such a sharing before, and feared it as one always does the unknown. Would my mind itself survive such a blending, or might I wind up maddened or ultimately in Xam's thrall, and useless to any further efforts on behalf of the Lady of the City?

As unpleasant as the options were, however, I found that I had very few alternatives. The surest path to the success of my mission (though even that was by no means guaranteed) was through this ordeal.   Doing my best to conceal my doubts, and very thankful for the lenses that filtered whatever Xam might try to learn through my eyes, I spoke directly to the little woman.

"My heart is easy," I said, "and my intentions toward your people are without stain. You will see that this is so, and there will be no more doubt between us."

She smiled upon hearing this, her permanently erect feeding teeth making that expression perhaps more threatening than she intended it. Waving impatiently at the other members of my party to give us room, she moved quickly to my side, taking my left hand in hers while offering her right arm to me.

"I shall not harm you, little sister," she said, eagerness leering from her small features, "for I see that you are as brave as the buffalo. Now let us see what there is to see."

The little pinch when her teeth stretched and broke the thin skin of my wrist was unfamiliar to me, for I had not been fed upon since my making. The rush of sensation that followed immediately, however, I knew all too well, and forced myself to latch onto her own wrist, lest I be lost in the song of her heart and thus unable to share in the sanguinary tete a tete that the procedure required.

I did not lose consciousness exactly. It would be more accurate to say that my conscious mind found itself within a plane of experience alien to anything it had encountered before.

How to describe it? I lived her life in a cascade of moments. I was Xam when, as a child still, she felt pride as she discovered her first of the little melons that oft provided her people with needed water. I felt her initial fear and pain in the marriage bed, and how that slowly transformed into pleasure. I am sure my breathing quickened, and that the rising clenches and trembles of that first conjugal orgasm shook my seated form, but I was her, and ignorant of what my abandoned body might have revealed.

I was with Xam through the unending agony of childbirth, and the greater hurt of the early death of first one child and then another. I felt the determination that had allowed her to channel that despair into knowledge, and how that led her at a young age to an unassailable role of leadership within her little band. With her clever hands I shaped bows and arrows, and painstakingly mixed the caterpillar-based toxin with which the points of the latter were anointed.

She was still a child, only in her teens though already a leader and grieving mother, when a raiding party of three

Matabele captured her. She had been gathering roots and herbs in the Bush, and, more eager than her companions, had strayed off alone. I felt her mindless terror as they took her and carried her bodily back to their cook fire. They raped her there, one after another, and I felt the pain and humiliation of it, their bodies huge atop and within me. They would have killed her after their pleasure, but she rolled toward the fire, a breeze blowing the coals into shimmering cherry life, and she thrust her naked hand into that wild furnace, grasped an agony of those embers, flung them at her nearest assailant, and fled.

I tasted the sick pain of those burns, and felt my hand heal, crooked and stiff. When, months later, she went into labor again, it was as if the cuckoo child itself wanted to tear her, and I must have screamed aloud in my dreaming, but she bore the infant, and with my hands she strangled it with its own umbilical cord, and I knew the hatred, hot as any wind-whipped coals, that she had cuddled deep in her little heart ever after.

When the vampires approached her she was already old, and they came (as I had surmised) not as predators but as supplicants. Their own little clan was fractious and weak, and they asked if she would accept the gift and lead them. Knowing that the skein of years available to her was drawing to an end, she accepted. The pain of her making was nothing compared to the agonies that living had visited upon her. And finally, though there were many other stops along the journey, I sat within her as she made treat with me, and felt the surety of her commitment when her word was given.

At the same time, and on a different level, as if perceived through a curtain that shifted with the air, I was aware of bits of my own existence as Xam picked over them. She lived through my own making, and knew how I had panicked, and fled and fought and wailed, when my mistress took me. I must have blushed then, in my abandoned body, but it was not the last blush it would be subject to. She tasted the blood of my first victim with me, and felt how I had almost cried out at the joy of that feeding.

Xam was with me when I met with Holmes and Rhodes and the Lady of the City, and she tasted of my gratitude and hubris when their request was made. She was with me, too, in my tryst with Selous, and sat astride him as he thrust and spent himself hot within her. From another world I could hear her wicked, gleeful laughter at this, and my abandoned body, beyond my control, must have pinked anew.

Finally, she read my mind when we had negotiated, she and I, and I am sure she found no duplicity there. At some distant level I was aware of her releasing my wrist and, though I clung to it greedily as any suckling babe, gently removing hers from my hungry mouth.

When the world fell back upon me its weight was at first unbearable, and I collapsed, only dimly aware as the Hunter ran to me and lifted me in his arms. Fixing the vampire with his unlikely eyes he cried out, "If you have harmed her, creature, you will not leave this fire. I swear it!"

Xam laughed at his outburst, leering at Selous lasciviously and touching her nether parts as she rocked her little hips forward and back. I think he might have been moved to rash action had I not struggled in his arms and stopped him with slurred speech.

"I am not damaged, dear Frederick, I said. "The lady was as good as her word, and I trust she will now accept that I am the same."

Thomas translated, and the little Bushman woman smiled at this, teeth glittering.

"Indeed," she said. "I have seen that my sister's heart is white, and I will lead my people to Iron Hill as you have proposed. We will not journey directly, however, for I have many mouths to feed. Instead we will find one of the Impis that also moves in that direction, and follow at their heels. An army leaves men along its trail as a poorly woven basket scatters grain; to illness, to fatigue, or to lingering too long with whores. These will be the rations upon which my people march."

I was by this time much recovered and, mustering whatever dignity the experience had left me, nodded my agreement, adding only one condition.

"Do so if you must, Xam," I said, "but when you reach the end of your journey you must sprint ahead of those that you follow, and so be in place to blunt the head of the Matabele spear when it is thrust at my people."

To this the little woman readily agreed. We divided what supplies we had between the two parties, and determined that, since the group travelling with the Bushman vampires had more bodies upon which to distribute the loads, Selous would ride Melissa and I my Coilcycle, allowing us to more expeditiously complete our task and, should it ultimately fail, rejoin the other party in time to face the expected onslaught of the Impis.

Upon those preparations being completed, we parted ways, but not before I subjected Xam to a fierce hug, in acknowledgment of the intimacies we had so recently and strangely shared. The little woman cackled gleefully at this and returned the gesture with enthusiasm, her arms around my bottom and her head barely reaching to my bosom.

As we set off, I suddenly realized that this would be the first occasion upon which the Hunter and I would be alone in the bush, sharing our little camps and with no other eyes from which to hide our activities. You can be sure I allowed my imagination full flight concerning what might develop under these circumstances, as Melissa maintained a sprightly pace through the sand and brush, and I, on my Cycle, whispered along almost silently at her side.

CHAPTER 20

Frederick avoids further intimacies—My protestations —I learn about the "Sea Cow Row" and its upshots—I plot at a water hole—A naked swim proposed—The Hunter assents to guard me—Attacked by a crocodile— A near escape—Passions renewed—A declaration of love—A romantic dalliance delays our progress.

It was soon apparent that I had presumed too much. The first days were uncharacteristically overcast, and we stayed long in the saddle to make good use of the darkened skies, which were far more kind to me than the sun would have been, and made do with cat-naps along the trail. On the third day, however, the solar eye rose hot and unblinked by cloud. I was disconcerted, then, when the Hunter removed the scraps of canvas from behind Melissa's saddle and set to fashioning not one but a pair of tents.

"Will you build me a fence, as well, dear Frederic? Or perhaps a chastity belt to better guard the remnant rags of my honor?" I asked, sweetening my voice to the point of toxicity. Selous, at least, had the decency to blush.

"It would be unmannerly of me to presume, Miss Monot," he stammered, daring a look at me before continuing, "and there is the matter of my own honor, as well."

I smiled, and made bold enough to stroke his cheek.

"An honest woman is a thing that I will never be, my sweet Hunter, but I see nothing in that fact that forces us to be more alone than we might be in these wilds that surround us."

The poor man received this sally with some distress, obviously fearful of offending me and, at the same time, thoroughly entangled by his own rigid sense of chivalry and the guilt stemming from our little escapade.

"But Miss Monot," he said, "the blame for what occurred between us is mine entirely. I allowed my lower instincts to gain control, and though I will always reflect fondly on the intimacies we shared, I cannot, for both your sake and my own, allow such transgressions to occur again."

I am no wanton minx, but neither am I a prude in matters of pleasure (and what woman would not be entirely flattered to see such a man in pain as a result of her attractions), and so I answered the Hunter in what I felt was a thoroughly rational manner.

"You can no longer hide behind the use of my surname, dear Frederick," I chided him, "for whatever the future holds the past cannot be erased, and we are beyond such formalities. As I'm sure you understand, I will never be any mortal man's wife, and will lay no such claim upon you, neither for what has been done nor for what might yet occur. Neither will I pretend, however, that such pleasure as we have had is dross and better neither remembered nor repeated.

"I am a Modern Woman, my dear, and not some bucolic maid condemned to wait upon the vagaries of swain and marriage bed. I gladly confess to my enjoyment of your caresses, and to my hopes that you will relent and offer them again. That said, I neither can nor would force you to do so (this was, or course, not strictly true, but it seemed the correct tack to take at the time). I will for now accept the lonely shelter you've prepared for me, but do not confuse my acceptance with surrender."

Selous' face was a perfect picture of misery now, and it was all I could do not to hug him. That would have been grossly unfair, or course, and completely unworthy of the subtleties I felt myself capable of. Instead I smiled, perhaps a little coyly, and slipped without further word into my makeshift tent, even going so far as to arrange the canvas to cover the entryway, as if out of a surfeit of propriety. My time, I believed, would come, and until it did I hoped the memory of my attentions would haunt his lonely bedroll.

In the meantime, of course, we had other concerns. My Hunter, who had a long and checkered personal history with Lobengula, did his best to educate me about the wiles and whims of the Bloodthirsty Tyrant so that I might be better prepared for the upcoming negotiations. Much of this instruction took the form of retellings of specific incidents, one of the most interesting of which he called "the Sea-Cow Row."

This took place near the end of 1883, when Selous, returning from the hunting veldt, diverted his track to the African King's city of Bulawayo to pay his respects; maintaining amiable relationships with that monarch being important to the success of any nimrod's efforts. As it happened, the Hunter's arrival coincided with Lobengula's chastising another European, who had attempted to profit on the demand for sjamboks by slaughtering a great number of hippopotamuses (the hide of which is used for these cruel whips). The sea cows, as they are called in that land, are of superstitious importance to the Matabele, and the Monarch promised that severe punishment would fall upon the guilty party. Lobengula greeted Selous warmly, however, and when the Hunter confessed that a member of his safari had killed a sea cow to provide meat for the trek, the King assured him that it mattered not and that there was no case against him.

A few days later, however, Selous found himself summoned back to Bulawayo, and informed that there was to be a trial of all of the white men then hunting in the area, overseen by a council of Lobengula's headmen. This prosecution lasted quite three days, during which Ma-Kwaykwi, one of these Indunas, accused the Hunter of being a witch who had killed all of the King's game, and demanded that he use his witchcraft to bring them all back, having them walk one by one through the kraal gate. At this Selous responded that he would gladly do so, but wondered if, when the lions came in, Ma-Kwaykwi would stand his ground to count them. This reply earned a good deal of laughter, all of it at the headman's expense, and engendered a hatred in him that, I would soon learn, had not yet abated.

The King eventually fined Selous for the one hippopotamus killed by his man, and the Hunter smarted under this unjust treatment. The next time the two met, however, Selous made to mention that he still felt he had been poorly used. The Monarch laughed at this, saying the matter was dead and that Selous should put it from his mind, and go off and "hunt nicely" until he could be happy again.

All in all it would seem that, though the past had not been without incident, Lobengula bore no ongoing ill will towards my companion (other than, of course, the currently developing war which found them on opposing sides). We hoped that their shared history would at least allow us safe passage into Bulawayo, that the Savage King would grant me (as a representative of Cecil Rhodes, whom he apparently had a high opinion of) an audience, and that during this I could attempt to make the case for peace.

That encounter was still some miles ahead of us, however. Another night of trekking ended with a clear morning, the sky unmarked by clouds and the day ahead promising to be hot. We made camp at a lovely spot near a little waterway which swelled at one of its bends to produce a beautiful pool, its waters crystal clear and, in the center, certainly five feet in depth. Here it was that I saw my opportunity to make my next move in the erotic chess game that I, at least, believed we were engaged in.

When Selous had established our camp (with the two tents which he had previously insisted upon) I announced my intention to wash the dust of the trail from myself with a refreshing swim before settling in to sleep. I further stated, and with a tone of wicked defiance, that I would bathe *au natural* to more fully enjoy the rare luxury of watery immersion.

The Hunter, as I had anticipated, objected to this plan.

"But Miss Monot," he chided me, "these rivers are thick with crocodiles, which, I assure you, make no distinction between a bathing human and a watering buck. And no matter how clear the stream, it is unsafe to assume that even now one of those horrid beasts is not eyeing this pool with a thought of breaking its fast on something larger than a fish."

"I believe you, darling Frederick," I replied, "But with you standing guard on shore, rifle in hand and eyes open, I would feel as safe as if I were in my bath at home."

"That, as you know, I cannot do," he said. "It would be most improper and expose me to temptation that no man should be made to withstand."

"Then you are faced with a difficult choice, my dear one," I countered. "What would you rather bear, the risk of my being taken by one of the scaly monsters and tucked in a hole beneath the riverbank until time and water season me to its liking, or the torture of having to look at me all unclothed?"

Here I suited action to words, and began to shuck off the cumbersome layers of my travelling gear. Selous steadfastly turned his back, denying me the opportunity to tease him with a slow undressing; and so I quickly divested myself of my garments (or did so as rapidly as I could, considering the tortuous underthings the age demanded).

"Say goodbye to your Paulette, sweet Hunter!" I called cheerily, stepping toward the water, "For I am off to dare the dragon in its den!"

This, as I'd hoped, was more than he could tolerate.

"Wait!" he cried, all exasperated. "At least let me fetch my rifle!" This he did, it being only a few steps away and leaning against a bush. With the Gibbs in hand Selous broke the action to assure himself that there was a cartridge chambered and then turned to face the water. "Bathe now, if you must," he said, trying to keep his eyes on the water and, indeed, anywhere but on my pale nakedness but, I was confident, at least occasionally failing.

So, in entering the pool, I sought to take advantage of those brief glances in order to capture his attention entirely. I am a woman of only average size, but I know myself to be neatly made. I stepped slowly into the shallows, bending over there to splash water on my face and present my bottom to him teasingly. I wet my hair, knowing that, when damp, its color changes from blonde to a heavy honey said to be quite enchanting, and dashed more water on my breasts before turning to smile and wave at him, my nipples puckering and hardening with the chill of evaporation.

At this point I knew I had his attention and, slinging my wet hair over one shoulder with a coltish toss of my head, I waded deeper into the pool, planning more deviltry.

Suddenly I heard him gasp behind me, a wordless articulation. I was turning toward the Hunter, inwardly congratulating myself on my womanly wiles, when I heard the rifle go off, the great cracking boom of it seeming to briefly suck the oxygen from the air; and from the corner of my eye I beheld a monstrous scaled tail lift once from beneath the water and slash down, beating the still surface to a froth.

I panicked then, experiencing an overwhelming, mindless horror that would certainly have been more familiar to my victims than myself, and charged out of the pool, knees high and quite forgetting to present my audience with a vision calculated to seduce. The Hunter had just finished reloading as I reached him, and I could see the great beast rolling now on the surface of the water. Selous took a careful bead and the Gibbs roared again, at which point the creature's thrashing slowed. The crocodile soon settled to the bottom of the clear water, which was only somewhat clouded by its struggles and, though surely dead, the monster continued to move limbs and tail languidly as its horrid muscles responded too late to messages sent by the now defunct reptilian brain.

What a picture of remorse I must have presented there, soaked and breathless and of course quite unclothed. An apology for my foolishness was already on my lips when Selous uttered a groan as if his heart would break and, dropping the rifle carelessly, pulled me to him and stopped my mouth with his own. Still in shock, perhaps, from the preceding events, I made to pull away but he only held me the more tightly and I surrendered, molding myself against him, my wet skin darkening his khaki where they met, and parting my lips to invite a greater intimacy.

Hands on my bottom, the Hunter lifted me against him, thrusting forward as he did, and I could feel the swollen heat there. When our kiss finally broke, her breathed words against my ear, like a torrent freed by a dam's breaking.

"Paulette, my dear woman, to think that I could have lost you due to my own prudery is almost more than I can bear," he said, his hands moving on my wet back and thighs as if they knew not where to settle.

"Hush my darling, I know, I know," I answered between kisses of my own. "But the dragon is slain and the princess is yours. Come; let me anoint you in the waters before we celebrate your victory in full." As I spoke I began leading my Champion toward the pool, undressing him as I did with quick and clever hands. The crocodile, its postmortem twitches now over, lay half on its side, rocking gently in the slow current. Seeing that it posed no further threat, Selous helped with my undressing, shucking the rough veltschoen from his feet.

Soon the Hunter was as naked as I, and leading him waist deep into the water I, amid many kisses and endearments, proceeded to wash him quite thoroughly and intimately. The poor man spent once as I did so, apologizing pitifully for this haste, but I was quite convinced that his passion and my attentions would quickly have him capable again, so only laughed lightly at his concerns and cleaned the spunk from his member, it drifting off into the clear water in thick, milky strands.

Another bout of kissing, during which I rubbed my breasts and belly against him and was gratified to feel an immediate response, and then I led my conquest (for, despite the unanticipated route my success had taken, I was congratulating myself for it none the less) to the camp and, collapsing the hated second tent with a single kick, reclined upon the fallen canvas with an air of invitation.

Of course he joined me there, and took me twice more, from before and behind, as I yelped with each thrust, both to voice my own pleasure and to augment his own. When he could do no more we lay entangled and sticky together and he stared all careless into my naked eyes (my glasses having fallen off at some point in the course of our couplings).

"I believe I have fallen in love with you, Paulette," he whispered, a condemned man's confession, at which I kissed him saucily upon the nose.

"Love me when you are with me, my darling," I answered. "For that is the only love one can be certain of." And when Selous moved to protest, I kissed him again, and rolled atop him, and for the first time slipped my teeth into his neck. In short order, the ecstasy of the feeding had empowered my Hunter to try for thrice.

Despite the urgency of our quest, we dallied for another full day at that place, and the sounds of our lovemaking rivaled the music of the night birds that sang in that setting of the sun. Those hours spent at this magical spot, which I've come to call "Happy Camp" in my thoughts, are the sweetest that I remember from my time in Africa, and I was to need the balm of their memory quite desperately in the days to come.

CHAPTER 21

Our mission resumed—A difficult river crossing—We encounter the Matabele—An armed escort into Bulawayo—Description of the city—"Calf of the Black Elephant"—My plea to Lobengula—Evidence of Rhodes' treachery—A second audience—"I am that fly"-- Ma-Kwaykwi rouses the Matabele against us— Selous' sacrifice—Blinded, I flee alone.

All too soon the weight of our mission resumed its pull, and as the afternoon faded we bade farewell to our little pool (which, the crocodile's corpse having attracted the attention of two of its smaller brethren, was no longer fit for bathing), and set out once more for Bulawayo and the hoped for tete a tete with Lobengula. Just as the sun rose the following morning Selous managed to bowl over a fat impala doe with a cracking shot at over two hundred yards, and upon her we both breakfasted, it being necessary to let the Hunter recover from my greedy attentions.

On the second day we came upon a strong river, which I believe is called the Umzingwani. Here we were forced to pause long enough to fell some logs (the riverbank being fortunately rich in sizable trees, the likes of which had often been rare along our trek), in order to construct a crude raft on which to float me, my Coilcycle and its heavy winding lever across the waters, with Melissa and Selous swimming alongside. Frederick and I (upon his direction) both loosed several rifle rounds into the water before crossing, to discourage any opportunistic crocodiles. Upon reaching the far bank, the Hunter informed me that we were now approaching the Tyrant King's village, and that an encounter with Matabele outriders was likely imminent.

Shortly thereafter, we did indeed come upon a small raiding party of that tribe, which was returning to Bulawayo laden with spoils, not the least of which were eight women from the village so plundered. These poor souls were driven in a line and chained together, with terrible iron collars around their necks. I felt an instinctual horror at their condition, but a glance from Selous bade me be silent, and he stepped forward fearlessly to speak to one of the raiders whom he apparently knew.

The party initially appeared aggressive, with much excited talk and violent gestures toward us with their stabbing assegais. As the Hunter spoke, however, these gesticulations became less frightening, and the raiders ultimately agreed to escort us to the town and there see if the Terrible Monarch would deign to speak with us.

Both I and my Coilcycle were the subject of intense interest from these individuals. It may have been the first time they had encountered a blonde woman, but it irks me to admit that my machine held their interest far more firmly that I. It was, Selous informed me, believed by them to be some sort of beast, and generally considered dangerous. Perhaps for that reason, there was ever a wide gap around me as I rode in the Hunter's wake along the road to our destination.

As we approached the outskirts of Bulawayo, it was immediately apparent to me that this was no village, but a true African metropolis. I won't hazard a guess as to its population, but Selous informed me that some 10,000

Matabele had been present there for the African King's coronation, and as we ventured deeper into the town I had little difficulty imaging such a throng occupying it. The news of the return of the raiding party (and of its success) had of course spread rapidly through the streets (though I use this term loosely) and alleyways of the settlement; and interest in this event was only heightened by the presence of the Hunter and me. He was apparently well known by much of the populace, though the expressions on the faces we passed made it clear that there were factions that regarded him with little fondness.

The city itself was certainly more than 600 yards in diameter, and roughly circular in conformation. The outer perimeter was demarcated by individual dwellings, mostly in the form of neatly made wood-beam huts with mud walls and thatched roofs, round in aspect, which sported firmly-packed polished clay floors. All of these structures were twenty feet in diameter or larger.

The dwellings loosely described the circumference of the settlement. The space within their border was largely open and, given the evidence upon it, was used as both a cattle enclosure and a drilling and parade ground for Lobengula's Impis. Also within the circle of huts was an "Indaba," or meeting, tree, beneath which Kingly proclamations were made and trials (similar to the one Selous endured, as mentioned above) conducted. The tree itself was an impressive old monarch in its own right, of the species *Papea capensis,* commonly known as the bushveldt cherry, which in season produces flavorful red fruits, the seeds of which also yield a fine oil.

To the southwest of the Indaba tree was a log-walled fortress, the Royal Enclosure, within which were found the African King's own dwellings, as well as those of his servants, wives, and closest advisors, and such outbuildings as were deemed necessary to see to the needs of this exclusive populace. It was to the entrance to this palisade that our guide led us, and advised us to sit in a respectful manner until he was able to determine if the Monarch would stoop to meeting with us.

This we did, and for the better part of an hour. (Selous advised me to show no impatience, as apparently this was common protocol, and expected of any visitors who sought an audience with Lobengula.)

My tolerance is not endless, and after spending a half an hour watching an individual ant carrying a piece of leaf across the sand beside me (and no, I did not attribute any metaphorical significance to this, I simply watched the ant), I was on the verge of standing and insisting to the Hunter that we return later, when we heard movement from within the compound.

Shortly thereafter our guide appeared, shuffling backward and bent painfully at the waist. In short order we saw the reason for his obeisance, as the Mighty Monarch himself appeared in the doorway, with his servant now supine before him. As he appeared our retinue cried out in apparent surprise. "How! How!" they breathed as if at a magical manifestation, "Oh prince of princes, oh thou black buffalo, thou calf of the black elephant."

Lobengula was a huge man, certainly more than six feet in height and, though weighing close to 20 stone, conveying the appearance of activity and strength. He was clad in very little, in fact nothing more than a chord around his waist from which hung a curtain of animal hide comprising all of his modesty, and a necklace strung with the teeth and claws of lions and interesting bits of stone. He was an impressive apparition indeed, but what surprised me most was the immediate impression of quick intelligence I read in his large, wide-set dark eyes.

"Selous! Why have you come here, and who is this woman with you?" His voice, though deep in timbre, was surprisingly soft for a large man of such bloody renown.

"This is Miss Monot," the Hunter answered. "She speaks for Cecil Rhodes himself."

"Rhodes," replied Lobengula, and I swear his tone was almost wistful, like a boy who is always picked last for team play. "How often have I asked him to come here to talk to me in person, and yet again and again he sends his cat's paws, and when they leave I find myself robbed."

I spoke enough Matabele by now to understand this exchange, which I believe I can translate here without resorting to too many paraphrasings. At any rate, the last moved me to attempt a reply.

"Good King," I said, curtseying prettily, "Mr. Rhodes serves at the pleasure of the English Queen, and thus is sometimes precluded from meetings that would otherwise be dear to his heart. I hope you will allow me to convey his respect and affection, and permit me to speak wholly in his stead."

The Monarch now turned his eyes to me, and again I was stricken by the perception, and perhaps even a hint of sadness, that I there encountered.

"I had dared to think Rhodes a friend," he countered, "and have been myself a friend to the white man, even when my people have opposed me in this. I have allowed missionaries into the very bosom of my city, and permitted Selous and other hunters the run of my realm. And for this I have been tricked into signing papers that give away what I never offered. And now my 'friend' seeks to force a war upon me and steal away my lands entirely."

At this outburst those natives behind us repeated their "how, how," but in a tone of sorrow.

"But that is why I have come," I protested, gingerly, so as not to excite his legendary anger. "Only show me how you have been wronged, and I am sure Mr. Rhodes will right it, and all bloodshed between our peoples can be stayed."

At this the African King grunted an order to one of his followers, which I was unable to capture the sense of, and the man so commanded fled quickly into the walled enclosure only to return with a small chest, which he set at his liege's feet.

Here the Monarch himself sat before us, though rather laboriously. I noted that, as their ruler seated himself, all of those in the crowd around us immediately prostrated themselves, apparently not willing to in any manner appear to be placing themselves above the mighty Lobengula. The King opened the container (which was approximately the size of a hatbox, though of wood and banded iron construction, and had, I guessed, been presented to him as a gift on some occasion, as it appeared to be of European manufacture) and gestured for me to look within.

"Here," he said, his huge hands touching the box as if it both drew and repelled him, "here you will find the evidence you ask for. In this chest is the full history of lies and deceit employed against me by white men." He appeared to grow excited, and removing several papers from the box, thrust one into my hand. "This," he commanded me. "Tell me what this is."

I examined the document quickly, anxious lest any delay on my part move him to fury. As soon as I began to read the agreement, which was in longhand and quite filled one page, with various addendums and notes scrawled along the border, I realized what it was, its importance having been stressed to me during my preparations for this journey.

"It is known to my people as the "Rudd Concession," I began, treading carefully. "In it you cede all mineral rights to

Matabeleland to Mr. Rhodes' British South Africa Company. Your mark is here on the bottom, and..."

"No!" the African King interrupted me, his eyes seeming to swell in his face and presenting a perfect picture of fury. "That is not what was said, Rudd spoke one thing with his mouth and another with his pen. He assured me that no more than ten white men would ever dig for gold in Matabeleland, and that they should come only as my guests. Here, here," he said, again digging through the chest, "here is a letter I had sent to your Queen explaining the matter." He passed a second document to me.

This was also hand written, though in a cruder style, and read as if the transcriber were taking down the King's words as they were spoken. This I read aloud, and reproduce it in whole below:

> *To Her Majesty Queen Victoria,*
>
> *"Some time ago a party of white men came into my country, the principal one appearing to be a man named Rudd. They asked me for a place where they could dig for gold, and said they would give me certain things for the right to do so. I told them to bring it to me, and I would see what I would do.*
>
> *A document was read and presented to me for signature. I asked what it contained, and was told that in it were my words and the words of those men. I put my hand to it.*
>
> *About three months after I heard from other sources I had given the right to all the minerals in my country.*
>
> *I called a meeting of my Indunas and of the white men, and demanded a copy of the document. It was proved to me that I had signed away the right to minerals of the whole country to Rudd and his friends.*

Royal Blood

I have since had a meeting of my Indunas, and they will not recognize the paper, as it contains neither my words nor the words of those who got it from me."
From Lobengula

"Yes," spoke the Monarch, nodding his great head. "That is the truth of it, and thus I wrote to your Sovereign, never to receive an answer. In this way the white men seek to steal my land, and Selous," here he fixed the Hunter with a baleful eye, "even he assists them, despite the courtesy I have shown him over the years. I do not seek war, as I know that many of my young men would fall in such a conflict. But how do I quiet my warriors when they see such evidence of perfidy?"

With this he heaved himself to his feet, shaking off the arms of the toadies who attempted to aid him, and indicating that, instead, these should gather up the chest.

"That is enough," he said "We will discuss these dark matters again tomorrow, at the same time. My men will find a hut for you to stay in, and serve you with meat and beer."

The provided hut proved to be a fine, sound structure, with a clean-swept floor and a hung kudu skin to serve as a door. Selous partook moderately of the millet beer and beef the Savage King had provided for our sup, and then, with our kudu-hide modesty curtain closed, approached me and placed his hands at my shoulders, apparently signaling a desire for intimacy.

For the first time, however, it was I who demurred, with a little shrug of my arms and downcast eyes.

"I'm sorry, darling Frederick," I said, "for despite our seclusion here, I imagine that every ear in Bulawayo would be attuned to the sounds of our pleasure."

He of course dropped his hands with sweet apology. In truth, however, though the presence of the curious beyond our hut certainly influenced my reticence, it mainly rose from a deeper concern. For I had heard truth in the Savage Despot's words, and in the evidence he had displayed, and for the first time I was forced to look at my exalted mission as little more than a small part in a decade's old betrayal. I would not, of course, turn away from the pledge I had made to the Lady of the City, but my impressions of my mission, and indeed of myself for the part I was to play in it, were sorely suffering in the cold light of fact.

So we slept, Selous well and myself fitfully, for Lobengula was not aware of my nature and so assumed that I would keep to the clock of the warm-blooded. When morning broke, I was thus grateful for my Terai hat, and for the garments that shielded my limbs from the bite of the African sun. Would that they could also have protected me from the events that would soon unfold!

The Black Monarch appeared at the appointed time, his retinue again bearing the little chest. As we had been sitting in anticipation of his royal arrival, he again lowered himself to the sand in front of us. After the cries of "how, how" from those who had assembled to watch us treat had died down, Lobengula spoke.

"This chest is filled with poison," he said, "no less so than if it contained vipers and scorpions and the caterpillars with which the little people taint their arrows. Rhodes, I fear, has always believed me to be an inferior man, and misused my trust time and time again."

Here I made to remonstrate, but to my surprise Selous stayed me with a hand on my arm, his pale eyes waiting for the King to continue.

"This paper," and here the African Monarch again produced his copy of the so-called Rudd Concession, "was obtained through a process that piled untruth upon untruth until the sun could not be seen above them. When Rhodes first approached me with his greed for our lands and gold, he did so through Charles Helm, a minister of your church and compatriot of Livingston and Moffat, for whom he knew I held affection.

"Helm presented himself as a man of God, and thus someone who would not allow his fellow negotiators to deceive me. Imagine my anger when I learned that this man himself was in the employ of Rhodes!

"I did not break off the discussions, however, such was still my affection for the white men. We talked for weeks, nay months, and despite their words twisting like a python with its head struck off, we eventually reached a modest agreement that I believed would protect my sovereignty and yet allow Rhodes to dispatch some few to explore the mineral potential of my lands. That was what was agreed to, and not the lies that Rudd placed in this paper and begged me, all unknowing, to sign."

The King fixed me with his great dark eyes, and intoned these words:

"The chameleon gets behind the fly, remains motionless for some time, then he advances very slowly and gently, first putting forward one leg and then another. At last, when well within reach, he darts his tongue and the fly disappears. England is the chameleon and I am that fly."

Upon hearing this, I cast a glance at Selous, but he avoided my eyes, and not, I think, out of fear of their power. As I was about to address the Savage Monarch to offer what reassurances I could (though I fear they would have rung hollow off my tongue), a voice screamed out from behind me.

"You see? You see? Selous is a witch, and he has brought his witch woman with him to cloud the King's eyes while they steal our lands and cattle from us." I turned at this accusation, surmising that the speaker was Ma-Kwaykwi, the Hunter's old nemesis, and further realizing that quite a crowd had gathered around us, whose intentions I did not at all like the look of!

In front of us, the King was struggling to his feet, this time allowing the aid of two of his attendants. He seemed about to speak, but a whisper from one of those assisting him silenced the Monarch, and with a last look that I thought rich in unspoken sorrow, he retreated into his enclave.

Selous had just slipped his Gibbs from his shoulder, and I was sliding my hand into my pocket to touch the reassuring presence of my pepper-box pistol there, when Ma-Kwaykwi bellowed again.

"Kill them," he screamed, "and we will send their heads to this Rudd. 'This,' we will tell him, 'this is the gold of the Matabele. And there is more for you if you wish it!'"

Selous turned in one fluid motion and fired a shot in the direction of my Coilcycle. This action served to clear a path through those surrounding us, and the gathering went ominously silent in the wake of the rifle's crack.

"Run Paulette," the Hunter said, already sliding another round into the chamber. And then the crowd was upon us. I ran, emptying the barrels of my little pistol into the first that reached me, and then counting upon main speed and strength to carry me to my cycle. These were almost enough, and no less than three warriors fell to my hands in my desperate charge, but a fourth managed a lucky slash with his assegai. I saw only a flash of light as it were swung at me and then the crude iron blade slashed across my face, cutting deeply and destroying both of my eyes. The pain half maddened me, and I fought on, my hands wet with my enemies' blood. I might have remained there, lost in mindless fury and tearing at my foes until an aggregation of blows finally laid me low, had I not encountered the mechanical frame of my steel steed.

Though in a perfect fury and quite blind, I still had reason enough to remember that Selous had bid me park it in such a way that it faced toward the road out of the village, in case we should have to hastily depart. I swung myself onto it, released the mainspring, and, the crowd giving way all round me in superstitious terror, sped off reckless into a world gone utterly black.

CHAPTER 22

Evidence that Frederick lives—An uneasy rest—My pursuer becomes my victim—A careening ride frustrates my healing—The scent of buffalo—An unexpected highway saves me.

I heard a pair of shots as I rode away, and took them as evidence that Selous had managed to reload at least twice more and was, at that time at least, still among the living. I soon had other troubles on my mind, however, as the road was anything but straight and in my sightless state I continually caromed off it and into trees and thorn bushes. The latter tore at me frightfully, and before long my clothing was in rags and my legs, or so my nose told me at least, were awash in my own blood. Such was my panic, though, that I continued thus until I could no longer hear the furor of the crowd behind me. Then, wary of the sun in my weakened condition, I forced the Coilcycle into a patch of brush, careless of my limbs, until I imagined it hidden, and slipped away from it, burrowing into what shade I could to rest through the heat of the day.

I never thought to sleep, but the body *in extremis* overrides the mind, and I awoke to the cool attentions of twilight and the sound of movement not far from my hide. The rest had restored me to some semblance of rationality, but my wounds, and especially the damage to my eyes, would be far slower to repair, and would take longer still were I unable to feed.

By the sound of the footsteps (for this they surely were) I was reasonably certain that my company was male, and almost certainly unshod. Thus I surmised that he was likely a warrior of the Matabele, perhaps having run some way on the distinctive spoor of my vehicle. If so, he was certain to eventually find me. Moving as soundlessly as I could while blinded, I got my legs beneath me and prepared to spring. A surprised grunt let me know that my pursuer had found my hidden Cycle, and provided essential information about his position and distance. With that knowledge, I screamed to startle him and flung myself at where I assumed he woMy y   My instincts were sound, and the first thing I touched was the shaft of the assegai that he had lifted before him in instinctive defense. This I struck away and, scrabbling sightlessly, was able to close my hand on his wrist. I twisted until I could feel the bone splinter. He shouted in pain, and attempted to push me away with his good hand, which allowed me to find that arm and break it as well. We fell to earth, he rolling to put his wounded limbs beneath him, and with a little growl of triumph I crawled up his shuddering body and ripped his throat out with my teeth.

Anyone who has gone too long without nourishment, particularly when the body is wounded and sorely in need of energy to repair itself, will appreciate the frantic joy of that feeding. He was dead when I left him and, though still blinded and half flayed from the thorns of the night before, I was in considerably better spirits as I felt my way to my cycle and rolled on my crooked and oft impeded way from that place.

It soon became clear to me, however, that I could not continue in such a manner for long. Though the recent feeding had rejuvenated me to some extent, the constant damage that my body was sustaining through my clumsy interactions with thorns, trees, and termite mounds was far outpacing my capacity to heal, and it was only a matter of time before my blind careening so damaged the Coilcycle that it would be unable to continue to carry me. Braking to a stop, I attempted to calm myself in order to better analyze the alternatives available to me.

This was not a cheering exercise. Though I had been riding for some time, I knew that, because of my erratic course, I was still far too close to Bulawayo, and that unless some natural occurrence erased the cycle's distinctive tracks it would be child's play for Lobengula's warriors to follow me. Selous, I had to assume, was either dead or held captive, and without his guidance I doubted that, even if I had my sight, I would be able to find my way to the rest of my party or, failing that, to friendly territory.

Of course I did not have the benefit of sight, and unless I were able to avoid reinjuring myself as I had constantly done during my flight, it would take days for even my accelerated powers of healing to repair the damage that had been done to my eyes. I confess to indulging in a moment of despair, leaning over my handlebars with tears tickling through the dust that caked my face.

As I sat there, though, I grew gradually quiet, and my mind slowly turned from inward to out, and began more carefully tallying the messages brought to it by my surviving senses. I heard the endless rhythms of bird, insect, and amphibian that formed the aural tapestry of the African night, I felt the dry coolness of the air on my skin; and I smelled on that small breeze, accompanying the more familiar scents of dust and my own blood, a faint sweet reek, reminiscent of a county fair cattle barn. The last of these nagged at me, as if there were a message there that I had yet to unravel.

Turning my face, I was able to locate the direction from which the zephyr came; faint though it was it still stung against my poor damaged eyes. I remembered the buffalo stampede I had fled earlier, and the bovine stink that had marked the veritable highway that the hoofed multitude left behind them. I was moving before the thought had quite solidified, rolling slowly into the breeze and toward the ever strengthening scent. Within minutes I realized that the aroma was no longer in front of me but all around me. It was not difficult, from that point, to sniff out the borders of the herd's passage, and to position myself between these. Once there, I rolled on, my manure-scented road guiding me as well as any London street signs, and was able to put some distance between myself and any potential pursuit without further injuring either my vehicle or my flesh.

After moving thus through the night, and feeling my way into a patch of shade for a second day's rest, I found the barn smell growing ever stronger, and before long could faintly hear the bellow and rumble of the herd ahead of me. I followed slowly, not wishing to overrun the animals and run the risk of a charge. When eventually dawn broke again, I was pleased to find myself able to distinguish the transition from darkness to light, and soon, by squinting my eyes fiercely I found I could make out, though far from clearly, the herd to the fore and the bushes that lined their pathway on either side.

I resolved to make full use of this improvement and, braving the discomfort of the rising sun, had before long picked my way through the brush and thus circled around the herd and set off ahead of the buffalo, following the path that it seemed they intended.

Thus with my eyesight turning and a mighty broom behind me to sweep away all trace of my passage, and with my Gibbs still securely sheathed upon my Coilcycle (for Selous had forbade my drawing it upon our entry into Bulawayo), I found myself still quite lost in what the wags refer to as "the MMBA" (for "miles and miles of bloody Africa"), but with my natural optimism rather recovered.

Chapter 23

*My abandoned safari's adventures—Xam grows bold—
The Induna plans retaliation—The Bushman vampires
become careless—One of Xam's men killed and another
captured—The Elder's revenge.*

As I was later to learn, the remainder of my safari was at
the same time encountering adventures of its own. From the
beginning my former companions had found their progress
slower than anticipated, as they stalked in the trail of the
first Impi encountered and the Bushman vampires reveled in
the unparalleled opportunities to hunt. As Xam had correctly
predicted, an army on the march loses soldiers like a hound
sheds hair in springtime. They fall behind from fatigue,
drunkenness, debauchery, or simple loss of enthusiasm. And
when these did so, the Bushmen were waiting, and fed to
surfeit.

Our little allies grew bold as a result of such easy
victories, and prophesized great successes in the battle that
loomed ahead.

"The Matabele will run like oxen taking the scent of a
lion," Xam predicted. Even Thomas, Michael, and Robert
(though still wary of the little men) seemed cheered by this
infectious confidence, and the mood of the small party
soared. Only Shaka held his council and his doubts close, I
assume so as not to poison this optimism

Such hubris, as the Classical Greeks teach us, will almost always result in a fall, and even as I was escaping Bulawayo, all blind and despairing, my safari was approaching troubles of its own.

They had perhaps worried the tail of this particularly Impi for too long, or simply underestimated the cunning of the Induna who was leading it.

It had been Xam's practice to send out her people, in teams of two, to follow in the wake of the army until they were able to make a kill, at which point she would replace them with yet another pair. Thus the Matabele forces were constantly harried, and the Bushmen vampires, reveling in blood, grew ever more confident. Such a strategy might have been allowed to succeed indefinitely by many commanders, who are so focused upon the battles ahead that they have little time or concern for what might be happening to stragglers who cannot maintain the pace. Unfortunately for my allies, however, this Impi was in the hands of Mjaan, Lobengula's chief Induna and one of his most formidable generals.

This commander maintained an enviable intelligence system within his army, intent upon informing him of any happening that might impact its readiness for war. Thus it was not long before he learned about the metaphorical terrier that was nipping at his Impi's heels, and at once determined to put a stop to this distraction.

To that end, Mjaan selected a small team which he instructed to drift back through the marching ranks in a natural manner until it was near the rear of the Impi, and there remain concealed among the stragglers, camp followers, and cattle drivers who make up that segment of the force. The Bushmen were experienced predators, however, and quiet in their work, so at least another pair of killings went unpunished before the inevitable clash.

Xam's own troop of vampires was, of course, relatively small, and it was not long before all had enjoyed the opportunity to feed to repletion. The little woman was loath to abandon the Impi, however, enjoying the opportunity to extract revenge upon the Matabele for past wrongs, and uncertain whether her people would encounter another army to so prey upon before reaching the rendezvous at the Iron Hill mine.

Therefore, she commanded a second rotation into the field. The fact that these Bushmen were less hungry than they had previously been might have influenced their carelessness. At any rate, it soon transpired that one of the pairs was sloppy in their work, and allowed their victim time to cry out before taking him down.

This was the signal for which Mjaan's rear guard had been waiting. The warriors immediately moved into action, forming in miniature the classic battle formation of the Impi; which mimicked the head of a charging buffalo, with the hard boss in the center and the two sharp horns turning the flanks. Thus was Xam's duo surrounded. The small warriors acquitted themselves well, leaving several Matabele bleeding out in the dry yellow grass, but they were ultimately overwhelmed and one destroyed (a ferocious stab with an assegai severing his spine) and the other captured and bound so firmly that even his unlikely strength was inadequate to secure his escape.

Xam was heartbroken and nigh unhinged with guilt when she received the news. The little Elder mortified her flesh with her fingernails and wailed terribly. Once her sorrow had been fully expressed, however, it quickened into rage; and she plotted to repay the Impi commander in his own coin, but with considerable interest.

The three warm-blooded members of my safari stood firmly against any plan that would involve a direct assault on the Matabele, who, in their hundreds, would surely overwhelm our small force despite any vampiric advantage. Shaka, on the other hand, simply refused to play any part in Xam's plans, clearly regarding the activities of the Bushmen to be beneath him. Though he too had taken advantage of the Impi's stragglers to feed, he did so independently of the predations of the smaller hunters.

All of them, however, were tacitly under Xam's control, since without her little army they had no prize to offer Rhode's forces, and far less of a chance of repelling the Matabele when it became necessary to meet the Impis head-on. The wise woman kept her own council, however, and the safari merely dropped back to follow the travelling army at a safer distance while they waited for her to formulate a plan.

The following evening, without consulting even one of her companions, Xam ordered the Bushman to move ahead of the Impi, a process which took most of the night, as a result of the size of that army and the need to circle well to one side of it to avoid detection. When this was accomplished, she established camp again, well to the fore of the Matabele, and it was noted that her people were unusually busy before succumbing to sleep, many of them hunched over the little stone mortars that are among their only tools.

Once night fell again, the little woman informed Thomas (apparently electing him representative of those not under her direct command) that he and the others had best move some distance away, as she herself would be leading the Bushmen on a sortie that evening and that "there would be troubles" when the Impi resumed its march on the morrow. With that all of the diminutive vampires left in a single body, following on the heels of their Elder.

I later learned that they made their way close to the head of the sleeping Impi, and busied themselves in a particularly thick stretch of thorn bush encountered there. As dawn broke, Xam presented herself to the waking Matabele, gamboling grotesquely, her teeth exposed and her empty breasts flapping.

In moments the warriors were awake and in chase, but were forced to push their way painfully through the thorns which the smaller Bushwoman navigated easily. Thus she quickly escaped their pursuit and led her people back to where Shaka and my staff had relocated their camp at her instructions.

Though my safari was some small distance from the Impi, it was within hours clear that there was trouble among its ranks. The entire army was soon forced to halt its progress, and the moans and wailing of the sick only worsened over the next day. I know not how many of his best warriors, those at the front of the Impi and eager for engagement, Mjaan lost to the Bushman's arrowhead poison that Xam's people had anointed the thorn bushes with. This gambit certainly did not rescue the hostage that the Matabele had taken earlier, but the little vampire Elder announced herself satisfied with her retaliation, and directed the crew to leave the limping Impi behind and head for the Iron Hill mine.

Chapter 24

Selous escapes the Matabele—Flight though a cornfield— Shots fired to signal me, but I misinterpret them— Cornered by two pursuers—Escape into the water—A crocodile drives him to land—Hunger and few cartridges—An eland passed up—Bushbuck in a snare— Food for the trail.

There is, of course, one more stray thread to gather in before I can return to weaving this tale. When Selous fired a shot to clear a path toward my Coilcycle, the roar of his rifle shocked the Matabele mob to a temporary silence. This was broken when I rushed to my vehicle, thus triggering an attack; but when I managed to reach the Cycle and blindly flee, all eyes were momentarily on me and my mysterious mechanical beast.

This distraction turned attention away from the Hunter, and he was quick to seize the opportunity. Knocking down the warrior closest to him, Selous took to his heels. Using his rifle as a cudgel (as he was reluctant to fire unless as a last resort given the difficulties of reloading on the run), he battered his way free of the crowd, sustaining only a slash across his left bicep, and dove into a corn field abutting against the city's edge.

The stalks, though their rattling marked his passage, shielded him from view and, while several spears did fall around him, allowed Selous to earn a few precious additional steps on his pursuers. The Matabele warriors are strong runners, but their abilities were not sufficient to allow them to steal a march on my Hunter, who had toughened himself with endless miles logged in the trek after ivory. Once he reached brush and could use that quieter cover to completely elude their sight, he was able to throw off the immediate chase and take account of his prospects.

Though not so dire as my own had been at the same time (Selous, after all, could see!), his situation was not calculated to inspire confidence. He was alone, and certain to be followed by some of the world's best trackers. The open wound on his arm was painful; although fortunately not too likely to infect, the rainy season and its bacterial soups being still some weeks away. Perhaps worst of all, he had but a half dozen cartridges for his rifle, a tree branch having snagged and opened his bullet pouch during his flight.

It is all the more telling, then, that as soon as he had thrown off his initial pursuit, Selous fired off two of those precious rounds as signals, both to inform me that he was still alive and to give me his location and approximate direction should I be attempting to rendezvous with him. (I heard these, as you know, but thought them only proof that the Hunter was still actively engaged with his enemies.) He was quite aware, of course, that ears other than my own would hear these shots, and so moved quickly away from the site of the last, taking what steps he could to confound those who would be looking to worry out his trail.

A few hours' walking took him to the reed-thick border of a small stream, at which he satisfied his thirst and refilled the small canteen slung upon his belt. He was still kneeling beside the pool when he heard a disturbance in the rushes and, looking back, saw the tip of an assegai wobbling among the tufted reed heads barely a dozen feet away!

Selous' first instinct was to stalk and overpower (either by force of hand or, if necessary, by gunshot) his pursuer. Fortunately, however, he hesitated and, still hidden by the surrounding reeds, was soon privy to a conversation which informed him that his enemies numbered at least two.

One of these was heard to complain that it had been some time since they had seen any sign of the white man, and since he had surely taken a different direction, they would be justified in returning to Bulawayo and relying upon the other teams that had been dispatched. One of these, the speaker reasoned, almost certainly had set off in a better direction and could be counted on to bring their quarry back to town.

His companion argued that his own assegai had drawn blood, which still stained its blade, that every hunter knew that a wounded animal will often make for water, and that the stream before them was the only nearby source of this lifesaving element. Thus the discussion went back and forth for some time, with neither party managing to convince the other. Eventually they did agree that they would be able to accomplish but little more with their stomachs empty, and so set about to build a small cooking fire.

Selous had been squatting motionless for some time, and as a result was in some discomfort. As the kindling began to pop and crackle, he took advantage of this noise to change his position and was greatly relieved. Still, it was apparent that his erstwhile pursuers were not about to quit the field at any time soon, as indeed the aroma of roasting ground nuts and bits of fat meat indicated that they planned a substantial luncheon. Some sort of action was surely called for.

As the men set to talking again (now apparently discussing the charms of some Bulawayo Belle whom both fancied), the Hunter eased himself into the stream, being careful to avoid a telltale splash and, holding his Gibbs and cartridge bag above the water and careless of the crocodiles that might lurk below, let the gentle current carry him away from immediate danger.

Selous drifted thus for some hundreds of yards, and might have continued further had not the sight of one of the dreaded saurians on a nearby bank argued for a return to dry land. Having accomplished this, and having donned the veltschoens which he had hung around his neck while in the water, he found that his thoughts turned to sustenance. The cooking scents from his pursuers' fire had underscored the fact that he had fled without any supply of food. The Hunter knew that he had several days of trekking ahead before he could hope to encounter friendly faces, and that the journey would only be longer if undertaken in the company of the specter of hunger.

There was little to be done at the moment, however, for even if he saw game, a gunshot would certainly help his pursuers refocus their efforts. So Selous set off, with one eye alert for edible fruits or berries and the other for vengeful Matabele. Not having to concern himself with my comfort, he determined to travel both day and night, and take his rest in the form of brief catnaps when fatigue would not allow him to travel further.

One such occasion saw exhaustion overtake him as he approached a water hole. It was, perhaps more accurately, a tiny lake, with one bank bordered in rushes and another in sand, and even water lilies adding to the picturesque nature of the vision. The hour was then just approaching dusk, and a fat moon filled the sky. Selous crawled into some bushes within sight of the pond and there, the sand still holding some of the heat of the day, drifted off to a needed sleep.

Some sound awoke him perhaps an hour later, and he beheld a troop of elands, each as big as a draft horse and washed mysterious by the white moonlight, emerge from the bushes opposite him and approach the water. Seven cows appeared first, ultimately followed by an immense bull, his body impossibly thick and almost blue due to the hair loss that inflicts these creatures with age. It carried an impressively long and thick twisted pair of horns, as well, and the nimrod in Selous was, I think, sorely tempted by these; but he knew that such trophies would needs be left behind, and found himself unwilling to destroy the great beast for the little of its meat he would be able to consume and carry. So, stomach growling cruelly, he rolled over and returned to sleep, resolving to make a starvation breakfast on starchy lily roots upon awakening.

The Hunter was rewarded for this abstinence on the following day. Moving carefully through brush surrounding a sand river (which would surely run in torrent during the rains, and even at the time probably held some lingering hidden pools), he was startled by a thrashing and bleating in the bush ahead. Selous was at first hesitant to investigate, thinking that perhaps he had heard a hidden leopard striking its prey, but his hunger argued for action and, as the noises continued with no sounds indicating the presence of a big cat, he held his rifle ready and slipped into the brush.

There he found a bushbuck ram of perhaps 100 pounds, its neck cruelly encircled by a wire snare. Wherever civilization has brought this material to wild Africa, whether in the form of telegraph cables or fences, some enterprising individual is certain to harvest some of it (with as little guilt as an English country lad picks an apple from another's tree) to fashion these most diabolical of traps.

The animal struggled mightily against its deadly harness, and Selous moved with care so as not to further disturb it. He also took a moment to study the snare wire for signs of kinks that could signal weakness, as a cornered bushbuck, though small, can prove a ferocious and even fatal enemy. That done, he selected a stout stick and, waiting for the buck to pause between lunges, brought the club down between its horns in a hard, two-handed blow. The animal crumpled, stunned, and a quick twist of knife blade found a gap in its spine at the base of its neck, killing it instantly without the need to hazard a gunshot.

Selous dressed the bushbuck rapidly, and chanced a small fire to roast strips of loin, which he devoured greedily, burning his mouth in his haste. Then, cutting a strip of hide to serve as a strap, he slung a hindquarter over his shoulder and set out again, regretting the meat left behind (which, he comforted himself, would in no time be devoured by Africa's ever-efficient furred and feathered sanitation squads), but grateful for the weight of food in his stomach.

Thus at least provisioned, he continued on his way, navigating by the stars and landmarks and by the incomparable map he carried in his head as a result of years of wandering the hills and plains of Africa, moving relentlessly toward the rendezvous point previously agreed upon. And I can only hope that, with his immediate survival assured, he spared some moments to indulge in worry over the fate of yours truly.

CHAPTER 25

My Coilcycle running down—Determine to push on—Spotted by Matabele warriors—A desperate flight—Bushman tracks in the sand, again—Desperate times—Xam is my savior—Reunion with my safari—Selous finds us as well—The Elder makes a prediction.

With my sight now fully restored, I was able to make good progress, pausing only to run down small bucks when hunger demanded, leaving them weakened but alive (though, I must admit, so as not to be said to be gilding this lily, that I knew they would be for some time vulnerable to whatever other predators they might encounter). I still had no clear idea of where I was or where I must go, but I was certain that Bulawayo was behind me and growing ever further so. For the moment that seemed to be enough.

I was not without concerns, however. Chief among these was my Coilcycle, the spring of which was running down, and would soon bring my motorized transport to a standstill. Without the winding mechanism, which I hoped and trusted Robert had not abandoned, I had no means of tensioning the spring other than rolling the Cycle backwards, which, since it would only store enough energy to return me to the place the exercise had begun, was no solution at all.

Thus I determined to husband its remaining capabilities by locking the spring in place and, walking, pushing the machine along as I went. This certainly made for slower progress than riding, or even striding unencumbered, might have earned me, but I had quite recovered from my injuries and had strength enough to do so, and was determined to reserve the Coilcycle's energy for that time when I might again require it.

"How! How!" I heard their cries of surprise before I saw them, as I had been trudging along and allowing my mind to wander, as one does when in the midst of a repetitive and weary task. That they were Matabele I knew in an instant, and though the tone of their outburst seemed to imply that I was not the game they expected to flush, I was certain that they would be more than satisfied were they able to bring me to bag. There were a dozen of them, each bearing one of the long Zulu-influenced shields of their kind, as well as a sheaf of throwing spears and assegais.

As they made their rush at me, I drew the Gibbs from its holster on my machine and fired, and followed that with all four barrels from my pepper-box pistol. Only three Matabele fell, however, as two of the bullets (likely those from the latter firearm, as the range was still a bit far for what is essentially a hand-to-hand weapon) had no apparent affect. With nine of my assailants remaining, and closing upon me rapidly, I did not like my chances in battle, for one or more might manage to run steel into me while I attended to another. Thus I re-sheathed the rifle and, straddling my Cycle, and hoping that superstition might slow my chasers, unbound its spring and leapt away.

The results of this action were, I fear, less than satisfactory. With its motive force on its last legs, as it were, the machine was capable of nothing like its top velocity. So though I initially did put some distance upon my surprised pursuit, the warriors were soon recovered and able to match my speed, running like hounds on a fox. My only chance, it seemed, was to pull far enough ahead to allow me time to reload my firearms, and that was beyond the current capabilities of my depleted Coilcycle.

It appeared that I could do nothing save delay the inevitable, and this I did with the baying of my enemies ringing in my ears. I was readying myself to sell my existence dearly, and preparing to bring my vehicle to a halt and face my fate when, glancing down to seize the brake lever, I espied a number of tiny human tracks crossing the sand in front of me.

Throwing the machine into a turn, its knobbed wheels flinging up a rooster tail of sand, I set off on the trail of those diminutive footprints. By thus changing my course, however, I allowed the Matabele to cut a diagonal and gain valuable ground. I could not tell from my perch how long ago the tracks had been made, but they represented my only hope, so I rolled on after them with my enemies drawing ever closer.

Eventually the Coilcycle could give no more, and even as it coasted to a stop I was vaulting from it and taking to my heels. I am faster than any warm blooded runner, and immediately stretched out my advantage once again, but even we are not without fatigue, and the warriors behind me seemed tireless and inspired by the inevitability of their success, while I was weighted down with despair.

I darted into a patch of brush, in faint hope of losing my pursuit therein, but it was fruitless. Already the first thrown spears were falling around me, and I slipped my teeth free and made ready for battle, when like a fever-borne apparition a tiny figure stepped out from behind a bush in front of me.

"How!" said Xam, in leering mockery of the Matabele, who were already pulling up in surprise, and then she and the Bushmen vampires burst from the brush and fell upon them like ants upon a grasshopper. What ensued was not to be dignified by the word "struggle."   The warriors were apparently unmanned by their sudden turn of fortune, and made to flee, but the wise woman and her people were in a perfect fury, and within moments the screams had died away and there was no sound save for the small people's lapping at the blood of the dying.

The little Elder saved the last for me, and though I had been feeding myself regularly on animal prey, I accepted her offer politely and was soon reminded again that human food, particularly when spiced with fear, in infinitely more delicious than the rank blood of the beasts. We left the bodies where they fell, the Bushmen only appropriating what weapons and tools their enemies had carried (save the shields, which were greater in height than the little people, who only gamboled about with these briefly before tossing them aside).

Their camp was not far away, and I was soon joyfully reunited with Thomas, Michael, Shaka, and Robert. The latter (who had faithfully retained the great cast iron winding mechanism, and apparently come to consider it his weapon of choice), I soon dispatched to my abandoned Coilcycle, to restore its energies and bring it forward.

There I also, and far less felicitously, found Melissa. That miraculous horse had apparently once again fled danger on her own during the uproar in Bulawayo, with Selous' gear still safely ensconced in her saddle bags. Seeing her, I was all the more convinced that my Hunter had fallen in the course of ensuring my escape, and I gave way to tears, only to find a small hand gripping my own fiercely, and Xam whispering a rush of syllables at me.

"She says you must not give up yet," Thomas translated, his own hand touching my shoulder timidly, the first such contact he had dared. "She claims that she would know if that particular ghost now haunted the veldt, and she has had no such visions."

I thanked them both (though I put little faith in such mysticism, being after all a Modern Woman). I straightaway mastered my emotions, or at least the outward evidence of these, and set about learning what adventures their party had encountered since I had left them on my fruitless endeavor, the results of which query are described above.

Selous found us that same evening. I was seated at a central campfire with Thomas, Michael, Robert, and Xam, a log serving as our chaise lounge. The remaining Bushmen surrounded us, in groups of one or more at small social fires that circled our own like satellites around a central sun, and Shaka as ever kept to himself. We had been relaxing thus, and discussing plans for the morrow, when Melissa, who was hobbled not far away in a patch of good pasturage, began neighing softly. Thinking that she might be alerting us to the presence of a predator or worse, I made to grab up my rifle.

"No need ma'am," said Thomas, cocking an ear to the gentle sounds. "The horse, she is speaking to someone." Xam responded with a lusty little cackle of a laugh and a rattled click and pop of speech.

"She says the horse is talking to your man," Thomas explained.

I jumped to my feet at this, just in time to see the Hunter stride into the circle of our firelight.

"Miss Monot again, I presume?" he said, and then I flung myself at him, careless of the eyes of my crew and Xam, though I knew there are few secrets of an amorous nature kept from the little Elder, and particularly none of my own after our recent bonding. When I had determined to my satisfaction that he bore no deadly wounds (the cut on his bicep already healing over from the good effects of sunlight and exercise), I kissed him soundly and lead him to the fire.

"I was fortunate enough to come upon the track of your infernal machine some miles back," Selous explained, "and rejoiced at that evidence of your well-being. I resolved of course to follow it until I should ultimately discover you. Imagine my surprise and concern when, shortly thereafter, I saw that you had drawn the attention of company of a different nature.

"At that point I began to run on the track, though it was clear that I was far enough behind you to make the odds that I would be able to offer assistance quite unlikely." Here he seized my two hands and gave them a hard squeeze.

"If I have read my trail correctly, it was quite a near thing, dear Paulette, though it seems to have been resolved in your favor!"

Thomas prepared Selous a cup of tea, which the Hunter received as if it were ambrosia and drank off with little groans of pleasure, as I described the culmination of my chase and the felicitous appearance of Xam and her people at the very last moment.

Selous held me close when I had finished my account, and kissed me softly, once over each eye. It seemed that our days of attempting to hide our dalliance were over, and I leaned close against him, thinking that, with the light of the fire before us and the star-choked African sky behind, we made for quite a romantic little scene. My nagging concerns about the English betrayal of Lobengula were for the moment silenced, but the pretty mood was somewhat broken when Xam pointed at my companion and spoke, her utterance followed by a decidedly lewd laugh.

The Hunter turned to Thomas for elucidation, and that worthy hesitated before providing it, finally speaking with his eyes determinately fixed on the fire and not upon either of us.

"She says this woman will break your heart, sir," he translated. "But she says it will be worth it."

CHAPTER 26

Lovers together again—On to Iron Hill—I confront Selous about English duplicity—A chill on our relationship.

If Selous was put off by the little Elder's prediction, he showed no sign of it later when, washed as well as cloth and bucket would allow, we celebrated our escape in the time honored manner of lovers reunited. We could not, alas, linger in this barren paradise. It was likely that there were other war parties still in search of us, and we already had ample evidence that the trail of my cycle, and indeed of the Hunter's shod feet, lingered behind us like a rope to pull any pursuers along. Furthermore, the combined forces of the marching Impis would, we felt sure, soon fall upon the little bastion at the Iron Hill mine, an isolated outpost that offered the best chance for a crushing Matabele victory and the subsequent inspiration of their hordes.

There was also another conflict to be dealt with, one that raged only in my mind, and I felt I needed to resolve it far sooner, as there were things that required saying no matter how much I, still in the blush of my reunion with my dear Hunter, dreaded voicing them. While the rest of the camp made our gear ready for travel before settling down to sleep, I drew him to one side and braced myself to speak plainly no matter the cost.

158

"My dear Frederick," I began, seizing his hands and studying his pale eyes through my tinted lenses, "Lobengula does not want this war, does he?"

I could see Selous stiffen at this question and, as if Xam's prediction had been turned upon its head, my own heart seemed to break just a little.

"The Matabele are a cruel race, Paulette," he replied, "they have long terrorized their MaShona neighbors, and while they are a force in this country the land will never accept the gentling hand of progress."

"Of White progress?" I replied, my voice small, for I already knew the answer.

"Where else would reform spring from, my darling?" he answered. "This is a land rich in minerals. Much of it is also well watered and richly soiled. It is destined, I think, to be home to English industry and agriculture, and a place where the stoutest of Britain's sons and daughters can, as they always have, dare, and strive, and succeed."

None of this surprised me, though to hear this admirable man speak such words pained me indeed.

"But is there not a failure of honor about this enterprise, Frederick? You saw the papers the same as I. The written words to which Lobengula put his mark are not the same as those he and Rudd spoke, are they? The mining concession is a sham and a trick, and yet still the old man has tried to hold the Impis back!"

Selous grew a bit cross with me then.

"Lobengula is no Father Christmas, miss!" he said. "His armies have slaughtered women and children. He has himself ordered his enemies staked to the river bank to await execution by crocodile. There is no place in the civilized world for such a monstrosity."

I slipped my hands from his, a deep sadness taking hold of me.

"He is but a man, Frederick," I said softly. "And what is monstrous in him has been in men through all the ages. Did not London itself, that paragon of civilization, give birth to Saucy Jack, he who carved up ladies of pleasure for his entertainment? The centuries to come will see worse than him ruling entire nations, I fear."

Selous made to take my hands again, and I allowed this intimacy, though I fear mine were limp within his grasp.

"We have but small parts to play in a great enterprise, Paulette, but I assure you our actions will save as many lives as they cost," he pleaded.

"I shall do as I promised the Lady of the City, Frederick, to the best of my abilities," I replied, my voice breaking, "but I tell you that this enterprise places a dark mark on us, one that will taint you for mere decades, perhaps, but that I will carry far longer."

I regretted it as soon as I had said it, and beheld the pain in his eyes at my direct reference to our different natures.

"Then at least we are agreed to move forward, Miss Monot," he said, dropping my hands.

We shared a single tent that night, but I think we were each no more alone when miles and miles of bloody Africa had stood between us.

CHAPTER 27

Encounter with an Impi—Matabele numbers daunting —Xam plays another trick—A Pyrrhic victory?— Return to our course—Romance rekindled in the face of disaster—An exquisite seduction—Shaka deserts us— Sweet memories defeated.

I awoke late in the afternoon to what I at first thought was distant thunder. Upon proceeding to the lip of the small depression that had sheltered our encampment, however, I realized that what I had imagined was a presage to coming rain actually foretold a different sort of downpour. The rumble that had disturbed me was not the voice of any cloud, but the accumulated percussion of countless feet upon a packed road, and the muted distant rumble of an untold number of voices. For what I beheld, for the first time, was the entirety of one of Lobengula's mighty Impis on the march.

My companions soon joined me, and we watched, each encountering our own wonder and individual dread as, for what seemed to be endless minutes, the great army wound its way across our field of view. I don't count myself an expert in the estimation of numbers, but there surely must have been upwards of 5,000 warriors in this horde, and the peculiar wink of the waning day upon blued steel indicated that at least a third of their number were armed with

Martini-Henry rifles in addition to the ubiquitous assegais and spears. When I considered that, to my knowledge, a force numbering in the mere hundreds was entrusted to the defense of Iron Hill, and that the army we were watching was only one of several which Lobengula could conceivably bring into play, I looked at my Bushman companions with new eyes.

I did not despair, for I had suffered enough to make me less susceptible to that most reprehensible of failings, but I did find the spectacle dire enough to cause me to determine that, despite my misgivings over the honor of our cause, I would not turn my Hunter away should he again wax amorous.

This resolution was interrupted when Xam, perhaps fearing that the sight of the passing multitudes might infect her own little army with doubt, spoke without turning her eyes from the spectacle, leaving Thomas to translate for those of us not her kind.

"She says to make ready to flee," he said. "She says she will put steel in the hearts of her men and women."

It is fortunate that we had already prepared our minimal gear for travel. Grabbing a bow and a small bundle of arrows from the nearest Bushman, Xam scrambled out of our sheltering basin and, ululating mournfully, rushed directly at the passing Impi.

The Matabele turned *en masse* at the spectacle, and some hundred warriors from the middle of the long line broke ranks to rush at her in a compact mass. This was apparently exactly what the little Elder had planned, for as densely packed as they were she had no need to aim nicely but merely let the poisoned arrows fly into their midst until all her shafts were expended, most of them it seems finding a resting place in the flesh of her enemies.

With a final cry Xam turned on her heels and fled, leading her remaining pursuers toward us, while the rest of the Impi merely paused, perhaps content to rest their bodies and watch the drama play out before them. Selous, Thomas, Robert and I promptly took to horse and cycle and Shank's mare, but Xam's people, and Shaka too, merely drifted into the adjoining bush and stowed their burdens there.

Despite her stature, Xam seemed able to maintain her lead over the pursuing warriors, to the point of apparently pretending a stumble now and then to keep their blood warm. When her pursuers had passed through our former camp, a portion of the Bushmen revealed themselves at the enemy's back and set upon them with arrows, teeth, and captured weapons before the larger warriors recognized this new threat and turned to meet it.

When they did, however, the rest of the Bushmen fell upon this new rear flank and, as their compatriots had before, stung the Matabeles' backs with poisoned arrows. Shaka too entered into the fray, the bloodlust quite upon him, and went through his enemies like a wolf through a flock of sheep, and from our distance Selous and I saluted them with a withering rain of fire from our rifles. In less time than it takes to transcribe it, the warriors whom had left their ranks to pursue the little Elder were dead or dying, and the Bushmen even took time to collect their own spent arrows before the rest of the Impi, realizing what had happened, came for us with a roar. These we quickly outdistanced, and it was a pleasure indeed (if not a little humorous) to see the strut in Xam's footsteps after this display of Pygmy strategy.

Because the skies were clear, and there was moon enough, we were able to travel through the night. At first we moved directly away from the Impi, until Xam, who sent scouts back to learn the army's intent, determined that there had been no pursuit. More likely, she told us with a cackle of satisfaction, the Induna had forbid any further breaking of ranks, and threatened his warriors with severe punishment should any presume to do so. (And when an Induna warns of such repercussions, you can be sure that the price of disobedience will be steep indeed!)

Once we were free from fear of being followed, we set our course parallel to the Impi's line of march and soon outdistanced it, our little party being far more agile than the great winding snake of that army. By sunrise, Xam and Selous (who had assumed the roles of leaders of our group) were confident that the Matabele would be unable to overtake us in a single march, and decided that we could safely rest through the heat of the day.

We had water and biltong enough for the Hunter, Thomas, Michael, and Robert; and the kin among us (myself included, as I had by now thrown off all pretense) had supped well, if hurriedly, on the spoils of our little skirmish, so once the former had discussed a frugal dinner we established a light camp and sought sweet regeneration in the arms of Morpheus.

That is, most of us did so. I noticed that Xam, ancient though she appeared, led one of her warriors off into the brush with a lascivious giggle, apparently rejuvenated by her success in battle and perhaps by the memories she had tapped into during our joining. My Hunter, I think still stinging from our recent contretemps, erected a pair of tents as he had in the past. I would have none of that, though, and wordlessly kicked at the stakes of one of these until it toppled, and used its canvas to better secure the privacy of the other, which I entered.

Selous soon joined me there, and immediately sought to reopen the discussion, apparently with an eye to secure my forgiveness.

"Dear Paulette," he began, "I am but a simple hunter, and not a man who presumes to judge those who move the chess pieces of this world...."

I stopped him with a finger to his lips.

"Shhhh Frederick," I said, "it is of no matter. Despite what you know me to be, I am still young, and likely naïve. It was unfair of me to blame you, who serves his masters as I must my Mistress. We both saw the size of Lobengula's Impi, and it is surely only one of the hammers the African Despot will swing down upon Iron Hill. Whether his cause is righteous or no, I believe that you were correct in doubting the ability of Xam's followers to turn the tide of the battle to come. It seems likely that one or both of us will fall there, so let us take what joy we can now, so we do not die regretting the cup not drunk or the fruit untasted."

"My darling," he murmured in reply, and made to kiss me, but I pushed him away gently.

"Not yet, my hero," I whispered, my own voice throaty in anticipation of the pleasures to come. "You have never yet undressed me. I want you to do so now, and slowly, as a connoisseur addresses a meal patiently, the better to prolong its enjoyment, and not like a spoiled little lord on Christmas morning, who tears at the wrappers of the second gift before he has played with the first." So saying, I reclined upon our canvas floor, careful to let my hair array itself in a golden halo around my head.

How his fingers trembled at my buttons! It was all I could do to heed my own injunction and not urge him to hurry! My jacket went first, and I sat up to shuck it from my shoulders, and then my blouse. I suffered him to kiss my bare neck then, before slipping my chemise over my shoulders and fumbling with the hooks on my corset. Finally the Hunter was able to remove that instrument of torture from me, freeing my breasts. My own fever rising, I taught him how to worship these, with hands and lips and tongue, until I could no longer restrain the little gasps that escaped me as I held his head to my bosom.

"The rest," I breathed, "remove the rest."

With a groan he unbuttoned my skirt, pulling it from me as I raised my legs to assist him, and then, while I was in that position, worked my bloomers over my hips and peeled them away. When I was fully unclothed I lay back, turned half to my side, and struck a pose intended to display my assets to maximum effect. Oh how he devoured me with his eyes! But when his hands went to the buttons of his trousers I stopped him again.

"No, my darling," I cautioned him. "It will be my chore to undress you when the time comes, but first you must learn to play with the package you've opened!"

It was clear to me from our earlier lovemaking that my dear Frederick was not new to the arms of a woman. He had, after all, been years alone in Africa, and it would be miraculous indeed (if not a sign of abnormality) if he had not occasionally succumbed to the charms of one of those Nubian Cleopatras whom, from what I had occasion to observe, were seldom better than they had to be! I was certain that such incidents were, however, hurried and heated things, as is the fashion of men who, through a lack of understanding, chase their own quick satisfaction and assume that what is good for the gander is good for the goose, as it were. Thus I was determined that, should he live to bed another, she would reap the benefits of his time with Paulette Monot.

Reclining, I let my knees fall to the side and, with my index and second finger, gently parted my nether lips. With my free hand I took his and drew it along there, letting him feel the wet of my readiness and appreciate its cool invitation, so different from the heat of a living girl. I showed him how to part the damp flesh there and release the little stiff button that every woman finds soon enough on her own. When he had done so, and began to pay it gentle attention with his thumb, my own gasps and trembles soon showed him its magic.

Once Frederick had thus driven me quite mad, I told him to do the same with his mouth and tongue. He hesitated at first, shocked perhaps at my perversity, but I persisted, running a fingernail over the still buttoned fly of his trousers, and he relented. At the first touch of his lips I was unable to stop myself lifting my hips to him. Emboldened by my obvious pleasure, he continued, tentative at first and then bolder, plunging his tongue deep within me. I was crying softly now with the joy of it, and he, remembering where I had guided his hand, moved forward to find the key to my pleasure, pulling it with his lips, circling it with his tongue, and nipping gently at it until I could hold myself no longer and, pinning his head there with my closing thighs, gave in to the waves and trembles of total joy.

My lover was quite in awe of his own powers as the orgasm shook me, and once I recovered (gently pushing his head away as I could simply bear no more), I set about his unclothing. This was far less complex than mine, and soon I had him quite naked. I kissed his mouth, lingeringly, tasting myself upon it, and then saluted in the same manner the scars that thorn and beast had left on his hard, spare frame. Finally (though I knew he wanted me there all along, and it was all he could do to refrain from guiding my head) I reached his cock. I stroked this with my cool, clever fingers, while I mouthed the tight sack of his scrotum, and then ascended the shaft with a series of kisses, pausing to lick wickedly at the tip when I reached it.

The poor man was near to bursting by now, involuntary twitches pulling his penis tight against his belly, so reclining again, I urged him on to me and into me, gasping aloud as he plunged deep, and in a few strokes felt his hot release, gripping him tight with my inner muscles, my legs locked around his, as if I would keep him there forever.

You can be sure that our second joining, with lessons learned from the first, was far slower and more varied. At one point, while yelping and gasping as my darling moved within me, I thought I heard Xam's wicked laugh from just beyond the tent, but I dare say nothing short of a gunshot would have distracted me at that moment. When we finally, still loosely entangled, succumbed to a few sweet hours of sleep, my Frederick's new toy felt very thoroughly played with indeed!

Sunset, and the sounds of our camp awakening, came entirely too soon. But duty must ride despite the whisperings of pleasure, and so we dressed (I thankful that I had never taken to wearing my corset as tight as was the fashion, and so that device was installed by the simple expedient of closing its buttons). I was justifiably smug, I think, when I slipped out of our tent, and able to meet Xam's leer (for it certainly had been she eavesdropping on our play) with a superior smile. It was only after we had broken our crude tent and were in the act of folding its canvas for transport that Thomas approached me with a hangdog look on his loyal face.

"The one called Shaka, mistress," he said, fearful as any bearer of bad news must ever be, "he is gone. He fled while we slept."

And so it proved to be. Of the vampire and his few worldly goods there was no sign.

This was an unpleasant development, indeed, and even my brave Frederick seemed stricken by it.

"He saw the might of the Impi just as did we, Paulette," he said. "I fear he was simply overwhelmed by the Matabele numbers, and decided it safer to brave a return to his disapproving Queen than to continue with us and face such unequal odds.

Xam was unaffected by this desertion, and heaped what I presumed were many a cruel word on the head of the departed, even moving her own people to laugh at his cowardice. But I was sorely troubled, both by the betrayal of one whom had so stoutly pledged his loyalty to me, and by the knowledge that we would go forward with one less weapon in our arsenal, and a formidable one at that.

I made sure to keep these misgivings to myself, of course, and sought to turn the discussion away from any contemplation of our loss by asking how soon we might reach Iron Hill. After some conversation with Thomas, Frederick announced us no more than two days' march from this objective. And so, with my recent ecstasies already seeming a distant memory, I urged our little safari to hoist its burdens (both psychological and physical) and trek on toward that uncertain destiny.

CHAPTER 28

A mysterious sighting—Xam's scouts investigate—A "ghost" ox cart—A disturbing vision—Unpacking the wagon—An unexpected bounty—A fright, and then a celebration—Forward into the unknown.

We were well into our first day's trek; just, in fact, beginning to look for an appropriate place to make camp as morning leapt upon us with all of its tropical urgency, when Thomas, walking at the front of our little column, suddenly signaled a halt. Frederick (mounted on Melissa now) and Xam soon joined him, which led to long studies by the trio of something in the distance, hands over their eyes, and a complicated trilingual debate. Soon I could bear the tension no longer and so hied myself to their sides to see this mysterious wonder for myself.

"There, Paulette," the Hunter said, extending his arm to indicate a spot on the far horizon. I stared till my eyes watered in the morning light, and finally discerned a long, twisted object, all but invisible there, like a tiny scarlet centipede almost lost on red clay. I squinted at the thing for long moments, but I was still unsure of what I was seeing.

"It's moving, Frederick," I said. "What is it?"

"Unless I miss my guess, my dear, it is a wagon, and pulled by a team of six or eight oxen," he said. "Very likely

170

hoping to find its way to Iron Hill as we are, with supplies or reinforcements for the garrison."

Xam, who seemed to benefit from the incredible facility with languages that I was finding to be the rule rather than the exception among my African allies, apparently understood this bit of English well enough, though she either would not or could not speak it. She replied with a cacophony of clicks and guttural rattles.

"She says we should hurry to it," Thomas explained, "and join our fortunes with those of the wagon's owners."

But Selous only studied the distant object longer, and I wondered if in this proficiency his eyes, by either birth or training, were actually superior to my own.

"I think not just yet," he finally said. "It would not be beyond Lobengula's forces to capture such a wagon and set it out for bait, with an Impi following hidden in the hills to either side of it. We will wait here. Xam, would you send two of your people to loop well around and come in to the conveyance from the sides? It is only by doing so, I think, that we can assure ourselves that a frontal approach is prudent." This the little elder, seemingly glad for an opportunity to demonstrate her leadership and her people's efficacy, promptly did.

It was certainly more than an hour later when we first caught sight of the Bushman scouts making their way back to our position. Even before we were able to distinguish details of their faces, the eagerness of their actions seemed to imply that they had discovered something interesting in the extreme.

By the time they came within hailing distance our curiosity was thoroughly engaged, and so all non-Bushman eyes were on Thomas as the first reports were shouted out to Xam.

"They say no Matabele, no white men, no men at all with the wagon," he reported. "They say the oxen trek alone."

Digesting this news, I looked to the distance again. The tiny specter of wagon and beast appeared to have barely moved, and yet there was an air of purpose in the stretched length of the thing, however far away.

"We must take command of it then," the Hunter pronounced, "for whatever goods it carries will certainly be important to the men at Iron Hill." This earned a general murmur of assent. All of us were eager to investigate the phenomenon, it seems, either to improve conditions at the bastion to which we travelled or simply to explore its contents and discover what treasures might be hidden beneath its hooped-canvas roof.

As we approached the wagon, the oxen continued to pull, careless of our presence. I had a momentary vision of the cart and team as some sort of primitive organism which, denied its head, continues on heedless in the direction in which it had been travelling. Given feed and firm ground enough, I thought, these beasts might pull until the ruts of their wheels have girdled the earth, and keep on still, in their slow, stubborn, earnestness, wearing that circumnavigating track ever deeper and deeper. For some reason this image chilled me, and thus I was grateful when Selous leapt onto the wagon and, with a shout and a quick manipulation of the reins, brought the beasts to a halt.

While there were no people attending the cart at present, there most certainly had been, as attested by the dried splashes and puddles of blood to be seen on its boards and fabric. The trekkers had clearly come under Matabele attack, but something—perhaps a return of the survivors to the fray or the surprise appearance of a British patrol—had held the raiders off while the oxen made their leisurely escape; and apparently neither plunderers nor defenders survived the resulting skirmish to take up the trail of the slow moving prize.

And a prize it proved to be. In short order the members of my safari, to a man (and woman, for Xam, her feminine followers, and I were as avaricious as any) were busily uncovering the caravan's secrets. It held casks of both wheat flour and cornmeal, as well as salted bacon and bully beef. There was wine too, and ale and brandy, tea and tobacco. More important surely (though Selous and my warm-blooded companions were quick enough to fill a pipe and a cup), the cargo included ammunition for the ubiquitous Martin Henry rifles, as well as powder and lead, bullet casting molds and cartridge brass. Also pleasing was the discovery that one of the travelers had apparently favored a . 500 Express rifle (which we later found, broken, by his corpse) and had left us a goodly supply of ammunition for that firearm, our own stock of which we had sorely depleted. There was even a makeshift medical bag provisioned with an array of rough-and ready medicines; gauze and quinine, iodine, and the bush hunter's trusty all-purpose potassium permanganate.

Other goods there were as well, though of less immediate interest. Indeed, the wagon seemed to contain enough provisions and equipment to allow one to singlehandedly carve a homestead out of the bush and maintain it indefinitely. There were farming supplies aplenty, including hoes, scythes, shovels and even an iron blade for a moldboard plow all ready to be affixed to whatever wood availed itself; a small steam engine with several drive shafts that could be put to any number of uses; a variety of foundry tools (including a vicious looking blacksmith's hammer that Xam promptly claimed as her honorary staff and weapon of choice), and even a spare wheel lashed to the frame with stout rope.

There was clothing, too, and a number of bolts of simple and sturdy fabric. In fact, the recesses of the wagon (and the ingenuity of its packing called to mind my admiration for the thoughtful use of space I'd observed aboard the *Boadicea*) eventually revealed even thread spools and a treadle sewing machine, as well as a stockpile of tanned leather and the awls and outsized needles necessary for its working. In short, there very few of the necessaries for life in the wilds of Africa that were not included among, or could not be fashioned from, the bounty contained in this little rolling warehouse.

In short order Thomas had established himself upon the driver's seat and, wielding a long ox whip that was also found among the plunder, soon had the beasts pointed in the right direction (for they had fled aimlessly from the attack, and only by chance and an instinct to seek the path of least resistance had found themselves upon a road). Our speed was thus significantly reduced, for even a briskly walking man will soon pull away from a team of these draft animals under such a load.

The Hunter took advantage of this situation by securing Melissa to the wagon and riding within; where he managed to use the supplies at hand to increase our stock of cartridges for the big-bore rifles further still. I visited him several times in hopes of offering my assistance, but his habit of smoking a pipe (which he now took to with great relish after being so long without tobacco) in close conjunction to the casks of gunpowder ultimately proved too much for my nerves and drove me away.

We did, as I have noted, discover the bodies of the wagon's original owners. None of them were in uniform, but that did not portend much, as many of those flocking to the defense of the colony were drawn from the proud stock of local farmers and ranchers, and no more directly associated with any military unit than were the members of my safari.

We did pause long enough to provide each of these with a shallow grave, though we were not so delicate as to not first confiscate any working firearms we happened to find among the bodies.

While Thomas drove and Frederick devoted himself to assembling ammunition beneath the wagon's canvas tent, Xam determined that her place of honor was best located upon the rear of the vehicle, from which she could inspire her followers with what I can only presume were thrilling speeches, and which were certainly punctuated with the most ferocious waving and pounding of her smithy's hammer that can be imagined.

Knowing that the Matabele were surely in the vicinity, and that wagon tracks would be like chum to the sharks of the Impis, we attempted to secrete the team and cart in a small grove of acacia trees when we paused for rest during the full heat of the next day. Xam relinquished the wagon to Frederick and I for this period, though you can be sure she did not do so without a knowing grin. Alas the open-ended wagon provided little privacy (and less so since many of our followers chose to sleep beneath it to take advantage of the deeper shade there), and neither my Hunter nor I felt comfortable enough to wax amorous under such conditions. Frederick did, however, being well fed on bacon, cornmeal, tea and tobacco, feel strong enough to offer me the succor of his wrist. Interestingly though, I found that intimacy, which not many months ago had thrilled me no end, to be satisfying overall but comparatively quaint.

By late afternoon we were trekking again, with the Bushmen behind the wagon and I riding alongside the Hunter (who had apparently fashioned as many cartridges as the stock of lead and brass would allow), and followed by Michael, and Robert, to the fore. We had just urged the oxen through a steep-banked stream crossing, with much whipping and shouting, when Thomas called them to a sudden halt and directed our eyes to a distant hillside. A rising plume of dust there clearly indicated activity of some kind, and I grew nervous (quite understandably I think!), until we were able to discern that the cloud was raised by a troop of horsemen. At this discovery Frederick raised a "hurrah," and his enthusiasm was soon proved warranted, as the riders noted our wagon and hurried our way. They were, we learned, on a scouting mission out from the banks of the Shangani River, where a force from Iron Hill had mustered hoping to take the fight to the Matabele, and had been charged to locate our very wagon, which had gone missing en route to that outpost and would have been sorely missed if it had not been recovered.

With this escort to accompany us, we were now assured a relatively safe passage to our destination. At the time I experienced a great sense of relief at being so delivered from the wilderness. As matters would soon prove, however, our joy would be short lived, as we were simply being led from bad to worse.

CHAPTER 29

*Arrival at the Shangani River—The arsenal at hand—
Another mission entered upon—Lack of game in the
daylight—The lost wagon found—Repairs in the Bush—
A nighttime journey—Unwanted company follow us—
A ruse buys me a few miles—Racing for my life—The
power and perversity of the Maxim gun.*

The Shangani runs from a point north of Victoria Falls,
near the outlet of Lake Kariba and, crossing a tract of
wilderness with which it shares its name, intersects with an
old hunting road approximately 80 miles northeast of
Bulawayo. It is a font of some volume, and impossible to ford
along much of its length even during the dry season. When
we reached it we found a sizable encampment there, laagered
all 'round with wagons and consisting of almost a thousand
men, almost equally divided between Rhode's fighters and
loyal MaShona warriors, the latter eager to revenge
themselves upon the Matabele who had long been the bane
of their existence. The force was well equipped with rifles, for
the most part of Martini-Henry make, as well as the more
formidable Maxim, Gardener, Hotchkiss and Nordenfelt
guns, these latter being quite the height of current military
science. All told it was a force to inspire confidence, but I
tempered any optimism I might have felt with my memory of
the great Impi that had wound past us, and my certainty that

it was only one of several such that were even now approaching our position.

Our wagon was here offloaded, and its goods dispersed to some crude huts established in the middle of the encampment, before it was wedged in place amongst the other vehicles forming our barricade. The oxen, as well as Melissa, were driven into separate enclosures for safe keeping, guarded there by a force of MaShona warriors.

The horse was not to enjoy her sojourn long, however, for soon after our coming the encampment became aware that another wagon had not arrived, though it had been expected some hours ago. Selous immediately volunteered to go in search of it, with the aid of a small force of Captain Van Niekerk's farmer/warriors with whom he had been joyfully reunited since our arrival.

Wishing to do what I might when it was clear that the survival of all of us could hang upon the smallest effort, I requested that I be allowed to assist. Frederick, perhaps growing more accustomed to my stubborn nature, protested weakly that much of the journey would take place under the sun, it being just midmorning at the time. I countered by reminding him that I had clothing adequate to cover me quite completely, and put an end to the matter by calling Robert to fully wind my Cycle.

We determined that Xam and her people should stay behind, along with Thomas who might translate for them as needed. There was no need to expose them to the heat of the day, and it did seem that a mounted troop would be most suited to the work at hand.

Our route was to take us back toward Iron Hill, as it was from that bastion that the wayward wagon had departed. Major Patrick Forbes of the 5th Iniskilling Dragoons, who had shepherded the columns currently occupying the Shangani River camp along the same stretch of road, informed us that he was quite certain that his progress had been shadowed by the Matabele, though he was uncertain whether they as yet held any strength in numbers.

The trail was of course impossible to miss, having been traveled by many wagons and hundreds of hooves and boots, and we got over the ground quite nicely, even while maintaining a reasonable pace so as not to overtax the horses (and did I chuckle inwardly astride my tireless Coilcycle, most certainly I did). I was surprised at the shortage of game, in fact we saw nothing other than bird life. The difference in the presence of wild beasts was perhaps in part because much of my travel in Africa had been during those periods on the cusp of night and day, when the animal world is at its most active, and also, perhaps, because of the great activity the route had lately seen.

It was mid-afternoon before we came upon the wagon, which had suffered the inconvenience of a broken axle. The driver, a handy sort, was well on the way toward shaping a replacement out of a limb cut from a nearby tree. Frederick and several of our companions immediately leapt to his aid, and a functional substitute was hewed and in place within no more than two hours. This, however, put us well toward evening, and it became clear that we would be forced to make much of the return trip in darkness.

There was nothing for it, though, so we set out at ox-cart speed (which is considerably slower than a horseman's easy pace, to say nothing of a Cycle) with the driver wielding his whip sparingly. At length this worthy confessed that he could no longer see well enough to guide the oxen. My eyesight was quite up to the challenge, of course, though I had no experience in ox driving. The solution was to secure my vehicle to a pair of handy bolts on the side of the wagon box, and free me to walk ahead of the animals and in that manner lead them. The horsemen, then, had only to follow the wagon, an easy enough chore despite the poor light.

When the hour was nearing midnight, I became aware of noises to either side of us; the rolling of rocks and the occasional snap of branch, which I had not previously noticed. I called these to Frederick's attention when next he rode up alongside me, and he confirmed that there appeared to be a sizable force of Matabele keeping pace with us along both of our flanks. They would not, he thought, trouble us until dawn, but at the speed we were going daybreak would certainly find us still not yet at our goal. There seemed to be little we could do immediately, but my Hunter called the other riders to him one by one and laid out a plan to be implemented when sunrise was imminent.

The noises continued, and more than once I caught glimpses of movement on the hills to either side of us, enough to convince me that it was indeed no random raiding party that followed us, but a veritable army, perhaps even an entire Impi. And still they made no effort to trouble us, content it seemed to keep us under observation until dawn. So it was that, with little more than an hour until daybreak, Frederick and the remainder of my escort (save the wagon driver who had contrived to sleep within his vehicle through the excitement thus far), stopped and built a large fire, and immediately surrounded themselves with a thorn-bush skerm, on the theory that such activity would pique our foes' curiosity and cause them to focus their attention on the armored and armed encampment, which it stood to reason would contain greater prizes than an unattended wagon.

The ruse proved quite effective, and I, followed by the plodding beasts that had no inkling of the danger they were in, proceeded on into the night. A small group of warriors did detach themselves from the greater force to shadow me, but a few shots from my Gibbs, guided by my superior night vision, soon wounded one and caused the others to draw back to a less lethal distance.

There was only the barest trace of pink in the eastern sky when I heard several volleys of gunshot followed by the thunder of horses behind me. Frederick rode up to my side, accompanied by one of his companions who passed by without hesitation and galloped off toward the Shangani.

"They come, Paulette, take a seat in the back of the box and keep your rifle handy," he said, quite out of breath, and then shouted the wagon driver awake. "Now is no time to spare the oxen, my man, drive for the camp as fast as ever you can. We will engage the Impi (for such it proved to be) for as long as we are able, and attempt to buy you time enough to make it to sanctuary." And with no more than a wave he was gone.

The sounds of gunfire and the horrid cries of battle continued behind us and grew ever closer, despite the cruel whipping that the driver now inflicted on his poor beasts. In a short time I found that I could see our horsemen, rushing back and forth in front of the advancing horde, engaging them and then dancing clear like toreadors. It was quite miraculous that none of them were hit by the Matabele gunfire (for firearms this group had), but it was clear that the wagon itself would soon be surrounded, and those horsemen who did not flee would be doomed, as would I.

With the sun now molten on the horizon, we turned a corner and there was our camp. The warriors were sprinting to both sides of us, and I was giving them hot work with my Gibbs, but the race was entirely too close to call. The backs of the oxen were striped with blood where the whip had marked them, and the wagon bounced terribly over the road, its roughly fashioned axle threatening to give up the ghost at any moment.

But then the Maxim guns, which Selous' rider had ordered be moved all to our side of the camp, set up their deadly chatter, and the first rank of the Matabele fell; bodies torn and wounded, and screaming with shock and pain. Another staccato splatter of shots, and the Impi was sprinting to buy itself distance from the deadly automatic weapon fire. The wagon rolled into the laager, the horsemen close on its tail, and the warriors, apparently determining that it was best to wait for the rest of their forces to arrive rather than face the horror of the repeating rifle fire again, drew back and established their camp.

It is fortunate for us that they did so, for even in that short engagement fully half of the Maxims had ceased to operate, their intricate repeating mechanisms falling prey to the constant dust of the African countryside. It was to be a problem that plagued us throughout the encounter to come, and threatened to rob us of our sole advantage.

CHAPTER 30

A day or work and worry—Questions about Xam's and my presence—Sorties probe the enemy lines--At long last nightfall—To rest but not to sleep—Romance a casualty of the battlefield—A surprise predawn attack—Retaliation in panic—The Matabele retreat—Impacts of the action on our arsenal—MaShona losses.

After the recovered wagon took its place in our barricade, I made sure to unlash my Coilcycle and present it to Robert for a thorough rewinding, the better to be prepared should future circumstances demand its use. As I examined the laager that would presumably be my home until matters were settled one way or another, my first emotion was one of claustrophobia. For months now the virtually endless canvas of Africa had been available for me to scribble my efforts upon, and now suddenly my world had been reduced to a circle of ox-carts and the company of this frightened, if determined, group of (mostly) men.

As the day progressed, the forces of the Matabele surrounding us steadily grew, as groups of warriors filtered in to take their positions among their compatriots. Some of these we watched arrive, others we merely heard, and still others only made themselves apparent by their influence upon those that we could see, as the sudden and simultaneous diving of a family of puddle ducks might alert a farmer to the unseen hover of an eagle overhead.

Though my body fairly screamed for sleep in the face of the rising sun, I found myself unwilling to succumb to its demands. Our enemies were notorious for their preference for daylight war, and I was loathe to be unconscious should an attack develop. There was also the matter of the Maxim guns and our other automatic rifles, which needed to be repositioned to cover any potential avenue of advance, and where possible cleaned and repaired to assure that as many as possible would function when called upon.

There were, certainly, some questions about and even objections to my presence, and even more concern about Xam and her people, whose nature was made obvious by their eternally erect teeth and whose very existence played upon the superstitions of the troops. Frederick was strong in our support however, promising that all would be glad enough of our presence before this shared ordeal was over, and for the most part his word seemed enough.

We weren't called upon during that first day, however, though a steady round of sorties, usually consisting of a dozen or more horsemen, sallied out to test the Matabele lines and attempt to lure some portion of them into range of the automatic weapons and field ordinance at our disposal. Lobengula's troops were steadfast against such temptations, though, and whatever skirmishes developed were of short duration and well beyond the reach of our scientific killing machines.

Sunset eventually came, and with it the assumption that we would be safe from attack for the hours of darkness. Frederick fed me lightly, and urged me to try to rest even if sleep should prove impossible during the time my kin are destined to be afoot. I attempted to do so, making a bed for myself atop a little pile of canvas and blankets in the corner of one of the storage huts. My hunter sat with me as I did, stroking my head in an attempt to bring me peace. And as he did so I came to the slow realization that the long hours of sunlight and the constant fear had quite burned all thoughts of passion from me, and presaged the fulfillment of Xam's cruel prophesy; but gentle Frederick seemed unaware of this sea change in his lady love.

"You have suffered sorely under the heat of the day just passed, my Paulette," he whispered while he petted me, "but tomorrow, I think, we shall both have cause to be grateful for every hour we live to see after the sun rises."

I cannot say if I actually slept, but the avenues of thought which I travelled on while trying to bring peace to my mind did lead me to some imaginations of the most vivid and memorable nature, many of which I would be hard pressed to differentiate from dreams. Reveille had been scheduled for 5:00 a.m., in order that all should be awake and ready should the Matabele attempt the dawn advance than many of our commanders expected of them. It was not yet 4:30, however, when I was jolted from one of those lingering fantasies by the sound of gunfire and the screams of men and horses, and immediately realized that we were under attack.

The Matabele focused their assault upon our MaShona allies, moving forward in a sizable advance involving at least a thousand warriors, I think being all or most of one of the Impis that had encircled us. In the predawn darkness, they were able to approach rather closely to us before a nodding sentry called out the alarm, and our response was, I'm afraid to say, tainted with panic.

Automatic rifle fire and the large explosive shells from our seven-pound guns were poured recklessly into the night, while individual soldiers let off their Martini Henry's blindly, with no knowledge of what, if any, results such actions were producing. Reckless or no, however the barrage certainly did some damage to the attacking Impi (it could hardly have failed to do so, so close was the range and so compact our enemies). I also suspect that the sheer ferocity of the response impressed the Matabele as much as any deadly effect it might have caused, and after reaching to the very wagons that formed our fortress walls they fell back in retreat.

Once again, this caution on the part of the enemy played to our good fortune, for the extended and sustained fire had for a second time left the better part of our most effective weaponry at least temporarily *hors de combat*. And more tragic still, our MaShona allies suffered terrible losses in the early minutes of the assault.

Chapter 31

The conversations of soldiers—En vino, by Jingo—Selous urges caution—Morning before mourning—Paget on the attack—A splendid image—"Mind the horns, Paulette"— The stubbornness of heroism.

The rest of that day passed without further aggression; much, I think, to our general surprise. Despite the ever-present air of danger, it seems that soldiers, when there is brandy about, will always find something to celebrate, and in the evenings many cups are lifted to battles won and battles to come. This proved the case the night after our first clash with the surrounding armies.

I of course did not partake of the alcohol, but the air of impending doom had perhaps allowed old conventions to go lax, and so my womanly presence was tolerated in the "mess" with the uniformed warriors. One of these, Harry Paget by name, had apparently enjoyed the sort of career that allows a man to drink for free whenever in military company, and on our second night in the encampment he had obviously spent his reputation well and was quite loquacious.

It seems that, in addition to expounding on his military achievements, he felt obliged to alert me to his presence and the many advantages it apparently offered me. "Zounds!" he exclaimed, draining a glass and slamming it empty upon a nearby table before presenting himself with an obviously well-rehearsed bow, "I'd quite forgotten how splendidly a pale complexion suits a woman's charms! Lieutenant Harry Paget, at your service, miss." Here he, with a leer, a stroke of his elegant side-whiskers and a click of polished boots, bent to kiss my hand.

"Paulette Monot," I replied with a curtsy, removing my fingers before he could begin to register their unnatural chilliness, "and though I am rather a newcomer to this country I assure you I've seen any number of women whose charms outshine my own, though their skin might be as black as any Englishman's heart."

"Ho!" he exclaimed. "A Yank, are ye? And an abolitionist to boot, I'd wager! Well, Miss Monot, mind that you don't let one of those African beauties draw a bath for you, or you might find yourself becoming soup before you know it!"

"I draw my own baths, Mr. Paget," I replied. "Though after a steady regimen of biltong and mealy-meal I might quite relish a bowl of soup was it on offer."

"Hear that lads?" he bellowed to the toadies who had gravitated to him, "I do believe that this one bites!"

At that exclamation Frederick stepped over and glanced from Paget to me. Though he was some inches shorter than the Dandy, his presence seemed to put the big man in some unease.

"Is everything quite alright, Miss Monot?" he asked.

"Everything is lovely, Mr. Selous," I answered, slipping into formality for the occasion. "This gentleman and I were just discussing cookery, though I believe I would hesitate to sample anything prepared with a spoon that has seemingly stirred so many pots."

"She with you, is it?" the Hero asked Frederick with a slantindicular glare. The Hunter only nodded, reached out to touch my elbow with a hand, and met Paget's eyes with his own.

I know not what passed between them in that glance, but it was enough to cause the big man to change his tack. Addressing the room at large, he changed the subject to the predicament at hand, perhaps hoping to turn my head with a dose of blustering masculinity.

"What your Abo understands, y'see," he explained in a booming voice to all who would listen, "is a touch of British steel. You shoot a darkie with a gun and the rest shake it off. Just magic, don't ya know? Not man's work. But you stand toe to toe with one, cavalry sword to bloody assegai, and cut him down, well then his mates get the message soon enough,"

There were a few uncertain cheers following this outburst, but in truth it was at that point of an evening when anything said loudly will sound quite superior to a certain portion of the audience. Selous, however, who had squired me to the event and, though not a teetotaler, had been cautious in his consumption, felt compelled to speak up.

"I hesitate to disagree with so decorated a soldier," he said. "But it might be prudent to wait until you've wet your sword before you declare victory. The enemy we face here is a brave and cunning foe, and Lobengula has his own share of rifles, though I daresay they aren't wielded with the expertise enjoyed by the English and Boer colonists. Still, if you find yourself with a Matabele bullet in your lights you'll be no less dead, English steel or no."

"Ah, and so Mr. Selous is heard from!" replied the other. "We have all read of your exploits, certainly, sir, and I bow to your superior knowledge of the warthog and the porcupine. The thing is, Freddy me lad, even the great bloody elephants never shot back, did they? If we were looking to organize a livestock cull, why ye'd be just the man I'd call. But this is soldierin', don't you see; best leave the strategies to those of us with ribbons on our chests!"

Frederick only nodded politely, obviously believing there was naught to gain from conflict among ourselves. There was some muttering in the room all the same. Those who knew Africa were clearly getting their wind up over the airy dismissal of a local hero. Paget adroitly turned the conversation to his myriad amorous conquests, however (casting a limpid eye upon me as he did so, I confess), before the Hunter led me beyond the reach of such bawdy talk.

Reveille the next morning was blown at sunrise, as was the usual practice, and the growing light revealed that the Matabele had, if anything, increased in numbers while we slept. We were quite tightly ringed in, though all of our enemies were well beyond the range of rifle ball, and the thin fingers of smoke from their countless cook fires rose around us in gray wraiths in the damp morning air, as if we were also encircled by an army of ghosts.

I was surveying this gloomy view, and preparing to take my own rest once the sun had risen more fully, when I heard a trumpet call to muster and the bustle of horses in that particular stockade (for the cavalry animals were kept apart from the oxen, sheep, and cattle, and of course more jealously guarded). I confess I was not surprised (and even a little guiltily gratified) to see Paget assembling a sortie around himself with an eye to giving us a little demonstration of the principles he had been so recently espousing; though I wondered that he, in the lee of such a wet evening, could either sit a horse or remember his boasts.

He had pulled together thirty men, who, likely inspired by his reputation, had an eye on shared glory. This is not a great number in the scheme of things, but our garrison was so small in comparison to the legion of our enemies that any loss was to be begrudged. I saw several fellow officers attempt to remonstrate with the Hero, but he only sat on his prancer and sneered at their pleadings. Selous, I noticed, did not engage in this discussion, but sat apart, perched on a transport chest, looking to be quite involved with a bit of whittling.

Of the several Impis surrounding us, the army directly to our northeast had long been judged the poorest in terms of numbers, and it is in this direction that Paget led his horsemen. The chargers stepped prettily, and you could indeed see the sunrise strike fire on the cavalry swords. Ahead of them, the Impi roused itself slowly, like a lion disturbed at its meal.

At 500 yards Paget reared his stallion high, sword in the air as noble as any town-square statue, and gave the order to charge. Oh how those horses made the ground thunder, and I felt a thrill of excitement rise in my breast all unbidden as I watched them pound forward.

The Matabele answered the trumpet call with their own shouts, and, their Induna at the rear reading the field of battle and calling out orders as required, took up their formation and prepared to meet the attack. There were some 300 of the dark-skinned warriors to Paget's thirty chargers, but it was clear that the latter felt that the unlikely odds were only a path to greater glory.

And so it seemed at first, as the Hero drove his attack directly at the Induna, who lingered behind the center (the boss of the buffalo-head formation) of his army. And here the Matabele seemed to give way, falling back gradually before the hooves and swords of their attackers, though at least one horse fell to their thrown spears, and the rider did not live long after he was unsaddled.

I found myself watching the flow and ebb of the distant battle transfixed; so much so that I didn't notice that Frederick had moved to my elbow until he spoke.

"Mind the horns, Paulette," he told me. "Just now."

At first it was difficult to drag my eyes from the heart of the battle, where horses reared and sabers flashed. Gradually I came to realize, though, that when the long blades struck anything, it was likely to be the steel or wood of an assegai rather than flesh, and that the Matabeles who seemed to be melting away at the point of Paget's attack were actually moving off to the sides, where the two outspread "horns" of the Impi had by now almost enclosed the reckless English advance.

"Just now," Frederick repeated, and as a hovering hawk suddenly folds its wings and falls upon a tremble in the meadow grass far below, the outstretched flanks of the Matabele force turned as one and collapsed in upon the little mounted group.

Oh, but there were screams and shouts, the high panicked neighing of horses and the rattle of pistol fire, made small by distance. I felt strangely unaffected, as if I were watching a play from the cheap seats and had lost the track of the dialogue, but all around me a sigh went up, and when the Impi reformed we could hear the Matabele's cries of triumph, the jeers they directed at the fallen; and dead or dying horses and bright uniforms, forever still, littered the ground where the Impi's horns had done their deadly work.

Frederick threw the stick that he had been whittling to the ground.

"If any of us survive here I trust that some fool will sing Paget's praises for this travesty," the Hunter murmured. "But there will be precious few songs for the poor devils who followed him today."

The news of the victory spread from cook fire to cook fire among the hordes that encircled us, and everywhere the cries of triumph rang up. Though the noose that surrounded us had drawn no tighter, I think we all felt its constricting presence more immediately that we had before.

CHAPTER 32

Matabele trickery—Forbes fooled—Our little general—A rout of the Impi—Selous leads a cheer—Xam's pride.

It soon became apparent that the Matabele had more than overwhelming numbers; and that there were tacticians among the Indunas quite equal to the guile and subterfuge of any of the great European conquerors. They took a day to savor their victory over the doomed horsemen, but put it to good use. Just as the next dawn was breaking, a force of warriors, descending from a kopje to the south, cast aside their great shields and approached apparently unarmed, in a manner that indicated their willingness to treat with us. Major Forbes, who had by now assumed command of our force, was quite taken in by this ruse and ordered a cease fire as the Matabele slouched toward us in the uncertain light of dawn.

It was fortunate for us, indeed, that we had others among us whom were no strangers to strategy. Perhaps Xam saw through the developing charade, or perhaps her hatred of her ancient enemy burned so brightly that she would not shy from the opportunity to inflict another bit of revenge, whether her foes be armed or no. For whatever reason, she ordered her Bushmen into position. It was quite miraculous the way these small men and women slipped among the fences and rubble to advance upon the oncoming warriors.

Even I, who was no stranger to the elegant movement of my kin, soon lost sight of Xam's people as they moved from wagon wheel to sheep to sun-blasted bush.

And so it was when, mere yards from the wagons, the Matabele revealed their hidden rifles and rushed forward with a cry of triumph, the tricksters were themselves surprised. The vampires were among them like weasels in a henhouse, their movements far too rapid for such mediocre riflemen to draw a bead upon. The ingenious attack soon fell into confusion, with panicked warriors touching off their Martini-Henrys willy-nilly, and thus shooting their compatriots far more often than their small assailants. One after another they fell beneath the hands and teeth of Xam's people, and soon panic took their minds away and they fled, even dropping their rifles in their haste.

I believe the Bushman vampires would have continued their pursuit, for their blood was certainly up, but Xam called them up short with a shrill whistle and they obeyed, albeit reluctantly, only stopping to sup upon the not yet dead as they made their graceful way back to the laager.

Our allies knew not what to make of this, and there were mumblings and muttered prayers among the ranks as they realized what they had seen. Hearing this, the Hunter strode to Xam's side and grabbing her hand, raised her arm high (though even thus it barely reached his head). "It seems we have generals among us to match the deviousness of the Indunas!" he cried, and then, raising his free fist into the air, he saluted the little Elder with a hearty "Huzzah!"

Slowly first, and then rising like thunder, the cheer was picked up by the ranks around us, and in the center of it the half naked Xam stood by Selous absorbing the sound of her triumph, and her dark eyes glistened with satisfaction.

If most of the Matabele were stricken with superstitious horror at such a turn of events, however, there was one among the Indunas who knew exactly what he had seen, and who was even now formulating a plan to bolster the courage of his warriors and drive doubt anew into the minds of his enemies.

CHAPTER 33

Mjaan takes his turn—A Bushman captive—The mortality of vampires demonstrated—Xam's fury—A desperate charge—A thousand cuts too many—The triumph of the Induna.

The old Induna Mjaan, for it was only now that his Impi had finally wound its way to the rendezvous, was quite aware of what sort of creature had so disheartened his fellows, and he believed he had just the sort of tonic that could restore them to full confidence. (Much of this, of course, I only infer from events that I myself observed, though I am certain that my imaginings do not fall far wide of the mark.)

Mjaan was the eldest of the Indunas, and by all reports Lobengula's favorite, valued for the clever mind that he had learned to wield even as his corpulent body had stolen away the speed and physical ferocity that had marked his youth. His army took its position in the chain of men that bound us, the others moving to allow it place, and so made the dilemma of our encirclement more hopeless still. A command must have been given, though I heard it not, for to a man Mjaan's warriors set to drumming the earth with bare feet and spear butts, drawing the attention of all to their ranks.

There was a disturbance therein, then, and the mass of black bodies spit out a yellow one, smaller and cruelly bound.

Naked beneath the rising sun, the Bushman captive looked anything but fearsome, and that surely was the Induna's intent. Mjaan raised his arm, and an axe was passed, hand over hand, through the compact army behind him until he could grasp it. It was a woodcutter's tool, not a thing of war; broad of blade and crudely fashioned.

The Induna was elderly and gone to fat, but his voice, at least, had lost none of its power. "Men of the Matabele," he boomed, "horns of the Black Buffalo. It darkens my heart to see you flee like children from your enemies. Look upon this one, is he not the same as those who so frighten you? Let your eyes see that he can be bound like any man!"

The Bushman struggled against the ties that held him, but he had been blood-starved, and the sun beat wickedly upon him, and his efforts were pitiful things.

"If this is a demon," Mjaan bellowed, "is it not a tiny one? What good are his teeth now, when he is thus captive? Will his magical speed and strength not save him? Look upon him, my warriors, and find your courage again! For even like a man, he can die!"

Here he raised the axe and, with a grunt of effort audible even as far away as our laager, swung it at the Bushman's writhing neck and so struck his head cleanly from his body.

A hush fell over the field as the little corpse fell, and when it became clear that it would rise no more, a cheer went up from the Matabele, picked up and repeated until it rang all 'round us, a roar to steal the spirit from warm and cold alike.

One voice dared answer it, though, but not with words. Xam's cry was a cat's scream of wounded fury, and before any could stop her (though I believe it would have meant death to whomever might have attempted to do so, even if it were me), she was over the wall of wagons that surrounded us and, too fast for the eye to follow, streaking toward the axe-wielding Induna.

Mjaan's warriors, heartened now, rushed out to meet her in their hundreds, and when they did so the carnage was terrible to see. With her bare hand (the warped right one, unfit to effectively swing a weapon) and teeth and blacksmith's hammer, Xam carved her way through them, leaving a trail of blood and bodies in her wake.

The Matabele did not flee, though, and helpless as any one of them might have been in the face of the little Elder's fury, one hundred blades, even wielded blindly, cannot help but inflict a dozen wounds. And the Induna contained many hundreds.

We could no longer see Xam, just the parting of the army around her, and we marked with dread how that path of destruction showed that her progress slowed. There must have come a point when she realized that her strength was failing under a thousand cuts, and when self-preservation overrode her fury; for she turned, far more slowly now, and began to limp back toward our lines.

Still the warriors hacked at her, and still they fell, but fewer died now, and at last she was on her knees, crawling. A shout from Mjaan, and the Matabele fell back, leaving her alone in the field, in her broken struggle toward safety. The Induna himself, armed not with axe but a warrior's assegai now, plodded heavily toward her. There was no speed in his immense body, and so the pursuit unwound in what looked to us like slow motion.

They were still far beyond rifle range, and a shot was as likely to strike Xam as it was her tormentor, but I could not stand there and do nothing. I raised my Gibbs, selected the rear sight providing for maximum elevation, tried to steady my shaking (for I sobbed, and I do not think I was alone in so doing), and touched off a shot.

Where that bullet struck, I do not know, but it made no impression on the terrible tableau before us. Mjaan had reached Xam now, and she turned on hands and knees to meet him, though a child could have dodged her attack. The Induna struck her in the neck, and we could see how her little body twisted against the assegais' steel. Again and again the blade came down, and the old warrior was even forced to pause once, hands on his knees, to pant and blow until his strength returned. At last, with a final twist of the blade, he succeeded in carving her spine through, and almost delicately, pinching at the little twisted kernels of her hair, raised the head for all to see.

If the cheers had been thunderous before, now they seemed to shake the very earth. I would not have been surprised if the Impis had come for us then, and if they did I believe they would have overwhelmed us, so disheartened were we. But they still feared our Gatling and Hotchkiss guns enough, I suppose, to hold back. Or perhaps they felt no need to make such sacrifices, confident that we would fall soon enough.

I, for one, believed the same.

CHAPTER 34

The wisdom of the African Despot—Around the clock attacks—Selous the desperate gunsmith—The Bushmen chose a new leader—Thomas and Michael in battle—I lead the Bushmen—Desperate times—The sacrifice of the Coilcycle-—A smithy's work is never done --A glittering on the horizon—An unexpected entry into the lists—The battle's end.

Lobengula was a wise king, and no mere child in the ways of war. And though he had not sought this conflict, his Indunas had, most of them, learned their battle tactics at his knees before, and were more inclined to be meticulous than rash. Thus their attacks, which were to go on relentless for much of that day, were choreographed to break our will and exhaust our armory rather than overwhelm us in one swoop.

If our kraal of drawn-up wagons were a clock face, the probing attacks struck us first at twelve o'clock and then at six; next at quarter to the hour followed by quarter after. With each charge we frantically rolled and dragged the heavy weapons from one side of our fortress to the other, and after each such probe there were fewer of these still functioning to muscle into position to meet the next strike. So fragmented was the course of this battle, as men and weapons were moved willy-nilly from one flank to the other, that I believe it would be better described in a series of vignettes, which I will here attempt

*

Eventually Frederick was pulled from the barricades altogether. His years of mending rifles under Bush conditions had made him the best of our number at making one whole Maxim from two broken ones, and at flushing the hard clay of dust and gun oil out of impossible places. He sat in the center of the compound, a pair of ambient wounded fetching tools and breaking down actions at his command, and fed our weapons back into the fray. But never so rapidly as they left it.

*

When Xam fell, I believe the heart had gone out of me; I was all but broken by the thought that my undertaking, having proven so ignoble, could cause the lives of so many and still fail! I stood looking out at the enemy, arms hanging loose and the barrel of my Gibbs trailing in the sand, a negligence which Frederick, had he seen, would have reprimanded me harshly for despite whatever difficulties existed between us. I believe I might have been waiting for death, then, but suddenly I became aware of the fact that I did not wait alone.

It was as if I had gravity. The remaining Bushmen, many of them sorely wounded and struggling to heal, were gathering around me. I prepared myself to apologize, to join them in bemoaning the loss of Xam, and then I realized that the dark eyes, all turned toward mine, reflected neither grief nor rage, but a sort of hard determination that was infinitely more threatening than any mere anger might have been. They came to me, like ferocious children gathering around a chaperone before crossing a street. When all were present, one of them, the man whom I had once noticed the departed Elder dragging off into the bushes for amorous play, spoke, surprising me with his clear, if halting, English.

"Xam tell," he said, "she tell us when she die we come to you."

The little speech surprised me enough to shake me from my resignation, and I called Thomas to me to better respond.

"Stay close to me," I told them, straddling my Coilcycle, 'and you too, Thomas, we shall see what form of weapon we might still forge."

*

While Thomas was bound to my side to enable me to communicate with my new followers, Michael and Robert were left to wield the two double barreled Express rifles. Selous had equipped each with a pair of bags of the ammunition he had crafted in the rescued wagon, one containing cartridges tipped with soft lead and another with shells whose bullets had been hardened. He instructed them carefully to put the latter in the barrel fired by the back trigger, and to use only those unless the enemy was close. His thought was that the front trigger was most likely to be pulled in panic, and would fire the soft lead cartridge designed to do maximum damage at close range. Furthermore, if the more carefully aimed long-distance shooting was done with the rear trigger alone, the front would always be available should desperation call.

The two fought side by side, Robert at first watching Michael carefully to learn the finer points of operating the big .500 caliber rifles. When one of the hardened bullets reached the ranks of the enemy, it would typically pass through the first one or two it hit and go on to create further havoc still. Watching, one could trace the projectile's path and guess at the damage done. When the cycle of attacks turned to where my two warriors stood, however, the soft point bullets did horrible damage, often throwing their victims back upon the ranks behind them. Side by side, the two men continued firing like a single creature with four arms, although I could not shake the conviction that Robert would have been happier using the fine rifle as a club, and I feared he would have that opportunity before the day was done.

*

Finally we reached a point where, despite Frederick's frantic efforts, there was but one automatic rifle functioning, and that only capable of short bursts before it would jam, and the operator be forced to work the recalcitrant cartridge free from the blistering metal with bare hands. The Matabele had certainly been calculating the decimation of these weapons that they feared more than any other, and they sent the fiercest attack yet at our southern flank. It was here I called forth my Bushman troop, and sent flesh to stem an advance that there were not enough bullets to meet.

I on my Cycle, they on foot, we swarmed out to face the tip of the Impi, and for a moment the enemies fell back, their fear of the little vampires not completely driven away by Xam's murder; and surely the sight of me, blonde and pale and teeth erect upon my strange mechanical mount, added to their trepidation.

The Indunas, as I've said, were wise, however, and they had overwhelming numbers. Whenever one of my vampires would in any way separate him or herself from the group (as one almost must when grappling with a foe) they would mark three warriors to counter the little enemy, and in most cases that would be enough to bring the Bushman down.

As they thus whittled away at our force, the horns of the Impi had swung wide. I saw that they were about to engulf us, and that superior speed and strength would be drowned in a sea of flesh. Jumping from my Cycle, I pulled the throttle to full against the brake, and sent it careening like a reckless bull into the massed Matabele. Enough of them jumped free, or attacked the machine with spear or assegai, that I was able to rescue a tattered portion of my little squad, and retreat towards the wagons.

*

Meanwhile Frederick, bloody-fingered and wild eyed, fought with the ruins of our Maxims and Hotchkiss guns. I was to learn later, from one of the wounded that attended him, that he even took the name of the Lord in vain in his frustration and fury. Oh, how I would have laughed to hear that! At one point, however, he espied a glint in the dust that was everywhere, and dug out a small comma of metal. Somehow, in the catalogue of broken weapons that he had built up in his exceptional mind, he remembered a Maxim gun with a missing part of similar shape. He barked at a one-legged assistant to bring the thing to him.

*

The wave of flesh was threatening to break over us. Rhodes' troops, many of their horses already killed under them, stood shoulder to shoulder with the surviving MaShona and my Bushmen, with Michael and Robert, as the Matabele armies drew together in front of us like a great raised fist. I quite let myself go, and I believe even poor Frederick would have withdrawn in fear from the horrid cat-snarl that must have formed where my pretty face (and I only repeat the Hunter's descriptions, without boasting) had been. With a shouted command from Mjaan, who had apparently assumed command of the joined armies, the Impis attacked.

At first we held them, with nothing but ferocity and fear and superior shooting, but as warrior clambered over fallen warrior, while the dust grew thicker and the reek of blood surrounded us, our line began to crumble. As I ripped a throat out with my hands, I thought I caught the flash of sunlight, a momentary reflection, from the hillside beyond the Matabele, a brief glimmer through the heavy air.

Then I saw another, and another, and the Matabele in the back ranks began to scream. I didn't know what was happening, but I shouted encouragement to our line as if I expected a savior, and my companions bucked up and found the strength for one more effort

The screams were everywhere now, and we could all see the sun dancing off the hillside in dozens of semaphores as it struck upon things that gave it back. The warriors facing us turned away, toward a more fearsome enemy, and we assailed their backs mercilessly. A gust of wind cleared the dust and smoke for a minute, and treated me to a welcome nightmare, a vision I had never hoped to see: Driving into one of the Impi's flanks, warriors fleeing before him like sheep before a herd dog, was a tall, emaciated man in ill-fitting cotton garments, with sunlight bouncing off his blue-tinted glasses.

Shaka and his people had come.

Caught between this new horror and our stiffened resistance, the Matabele suffered terrible losses. Their ranks were massed, shoulder to shoulder, too close together for many of them to even swing an assegai, when Frederick, having dragged the single repaired Maxim to the edge of the compound with the help of his crippled assistants, began to hose the Impis with automatic weapon fire.

They broke then, first at the edges and then, as the panic spread like a rumor among them, wholesale. Like locusts across the sky, the dark cloud of the Impis fled. Selous, turning the Maxim over to one of his assistants, quickly rounded up the remaining horses and, selecting a number of riders, was almost immediately in pursuit, determined to harry them closely enough to prevent their recovery. The fields around me were strewn thick with dead and dying. The battle was over. Cecil Rhodes had won.

CHAPTER 35

The aftermath of conflict--A reunion over dinner—Royalty refused—The dance of Mars and Venus—A boast of bugles—What have I lost, what have I gained—A plea for home—A heart is broken after all—Poetic injustice.

In the wake of the Matabele retreat, the world around our kraal could have been something dreamed up by the poetic Mr. Alighieri. A mixture of gun smoke and dust smudged the air, caught precisely by the low afternoon sunlight. The air smelled richly of cordite, blood, heat, and acrid fear; and the sounds of the retreating battle, where our horsemen still worried the warriors to ensure the completion of their rout, provided a backdrop of hoof beat and gunshot to the nearer symphony of moans and screams.

Through those drifting sunlit clouds the shapes of Shaka's people, strange enough already in their poorly-fitting cotton clothes and the empty reflective eyes of their tinted glasses, could be seem moving slope-backed like hyenas among the corpses, only to pause at the still living and stoop further to feed. This was not the time or place for mercy, or for the myth of civilized morality (for had not civilization pushed the matter until only a resolution like this were possible?). So, calling for Thomas's attendance, I lead the remnants of the Bushmen vampires through the bullet-riddled wagons and onto the killing fields in search of the only medicine that would heal them.

Instructing Thomas (who by now affected a complete indifference to such a commonplace occurrence as blood sucking; final evidence that the human brain can accustom itself to virtually anything in a very short time) to inform the larger vampires that the Bushmen were to be welcomed or they would face my ire, I found Shaka himself, bent, as befitted his heroism, over the delicacy of a fallen Induna. Kneeling beside him, I cast a glance at his prey as he once had at an impala I had slain. He grinned in reply, his mouth red and black with blood old and new and his incisors streaked with scarlet, and pointed to the dying General, indicating his permission. I fed by his side; it was the only thing I could think to do that could convey my thanks and, simultaneously, free him from his imagined obligation. Finishing, I dabbed my lips on my sleeve, as primly as ever one can when cleaning another's blood from her mouth, and, with   Thomas translating, spoke.

"You shall always have my friendship, dear Shaka, and your Queen my thanks, for the deeds you have done today..." I began. But Shaka smiled again, lips pulled back from his teeth, and laughed bitterly.

"That woman, she who is no longer my Queen, had no part in this, Mistress, "he said. "She has grown cruel and jealous, and these men and women (and I only noticed now that the creatures he had assembled were almost evenly split by gender) have joined me in leaving her service, and beg you to remain in our land and lead us wisely and well."

I was of course shocked and flattered by this revelation, and took his hands, still sticky from their deadly work, in mine as I answered.

"Though I love you for your loyalty, and will always remember both you and this country for the things you have taught me, Shaka, I long to be in my own land and with my own people again. There are paths that I needs walk there, trails which I cannot follow here. These men and women who have come with you did so at your behest, and followed your lead without question. Perhaps it is time you put on the mantle that was promised at your naming, and became their leader in fact as well as in title. Furthermore, I would ask that you take these people with you (and here I waved a hand at the Bushmen who were feeding noisily around us), for they are more like you than unlike you, and the enemy you have defeated together has terrorized their village as it has yours."

Hearing Thomas translate this, the little people looked up, as did Shaka's, and he considered my words long before squeezing my hands fiercely.

"It will be as you ask, my Mistress. In return I only beg that you return to us one day, that I might show those who will later come to swell our ranks the golden woman who saved my life and made me a King."

"That I will do, Shaka, as soon as ever I can," I pledged, "for the world outside of Africa grows ever smaller, and time is a little thing to such as you and me."

With some trepidation, the two groups drifted together after dining, and once again I was reminded that Eros thrives on a full stomach; for after the initial uncertainty, there erupted smatterings of giggle among men and women, large and small, as they assayed their sudden increase in potential partners.

Perhaps it was this that sparked my loneliness when, after the vampires had departed together, I made my way back to the wagon-encircled kraal. There, as the sole representative of both my kin and my gender, I walked among the wounded and the wearied, those who worked frantically to repair our weaponry should our victory prove pyrrhic, and those who were determined to celebrate it with strong drink, the devil take the future. The former I did not aid, for I am no Florence Nightingale, and I was sore conflicted by our victory despite my own survival. Of the latter, I noticed many glancing my way with a speculative eye; for there are some men who, particularly when in their cups, will always see the woman in the monster, and disregard the monster in the woman, until it is quite too late.

Thus I ignored all and indulged myself in a brown study until, I know not how long later, I heard the braggart notes of a bugle call, and soon thereafter the distant chuckling of hoof beats.

Spitting on a clean-ish bit of sleeve, I did what I would to remove the signs of feeding from my mouth, and to cleanse my face of the worst of the battle grime upon it. My hair was pristine beneath my hat, and a ruin beyond it. So I only attempted to straighten it out as I might with my fingers, and in doing so dislodged the worst of the dust that had stolen its shine.

The horn, of course, boasted of the return of the horsemen, Frederick among them, who had pursued the Matabele in their flight. I probed my emotions fruitlessly for any sign of worry. Clearly I had either determined that he was too exceptional a man to fall in such a manner, or my feelings, which he had once commanded so effortlessly, had withered away at the vine that had held him.

It is not, you must understand, that I was indifferent to his return. Quite the contrary, I still felt an abiding fondness for and gratitude to the man, and was even gratified to anticipate the pleasure of his company again, but love, and lust, had fled. I'm afraid I mourned more pitifully over its loss than I would have done had he fallen dead to a Matabele assegai.

My Hunter, however, was afire with victory and fairly leapt from his horse when he sighted me.

"Paulette, my dear!" He shouted. "We were not able to finish the enemy entire, but we lay such a quirt to their backsides that we shall not see their faces again, I'm sure!" And he made to take me in his arms.

"I'm glad, Frederick," I said, and though my flesh is always chill I fear that the coolness it displayed in his embrace was far sharper still. He withdrew his arms, stiffly.

"Is ought the matter, you are unharmed I trust?" He said, as if ashamed that he had not first thought to ascertain my wellness.

"I am whole, and only filthy, and exhausted, and suddenly very tired of this place," I said, trying not to sound petulant. "The thing is done, I have played my role. I want to go home, Frederick. I want to go back to the world I was a girl in, and leave behind, if I can, this woman that Africa has made of me."

I'm sure the Hunter quite misunderstood this little tantrum, and assumed it had to do with our amorous tanglings and not the bout of conscience that blackened my thoughts. And I allowed him to think so.

We were offered our pick of the wagons and oxen, a noble recognition of our role in the already famous victory, but I churlishly refused any such favor. A cart, I felt, would be too slow to endure, and only a horse and my Coilcycle (wounded but still serviceable) would get me away from the Shangani River rapidly enough. Thus I said my goodbyes to Thomas, Michael, and Robert, bidding them to follow in our path; and assuring them that at the end of it they would be well rewarded and offered ongoing service with the Hunter.

Selous set to the arrangements with characteristic efficiency. It was determined that the most expeditious route would take us overland to Plumtree, which, though close to Lobengula's town of Bulawayo, had been spared in the recent unpleasantness, and from which I could board a train and thus begin my journey back into the Modern World. The poor man was clearly suffering from my air of pointed politeness, but I found I was unable to give him any relief.

Thus, after a night's sleep for the Hunter and a long day's rest for me, we set out well provisioned for what promised to be a trip of only two days. Selous was convinced the Matabele would be still in flight and were not likely to pose a threat; and that the two of us on horseback and machine, unburdened by hangers-on, could easily show them our heels if forced to do so.

Frederick rode silently for most of the first leg of our trip, only venturing into speech to point out this interesting specimen of wildlife and that unique feature of the landscape. We made good time in this manner, and at the end of a night's ride set ourselves a minimal camp at which to rest our bodies and for Frederick to enjoy a simple meal. (He offered me his blood as he formerly had, but I plead satiation from the spoils of battle, and thus denied him even that pleasure.) Considerate to a fault, he set up two tents as he had in our chaste past, and set about kindling a fire.

This was barely burning when a rider approached us, from a small group left in the field to report on the Matabele rout. He informed us in some excitement that Lobengula had put his city to the torch and fled, a loyal Impi still covering his retreat. I sat in quiet politeness as Frederick provided the rider with a cup of tea and a plate of stewed biltong, and only when the scout had ridden off (perhaps wondering why we were camped in full daylight), did I finally give in to my emotions and collapse in wracking tears.

"My girl!" Frederick exclaimed, laying a hesitant hand on my shoulder, "whatever is wrong?"

I sobbed quite pathetically I'm afraid.

"I'm wrong, Frederick. We're wrong. It's all wrong. They will kill that poor man won't they? Oh I know he was horribly cruel, but in this instance he was in the right. He tried to civilize himself, but he could see not see behind the trappings of civilization, and only too late understood that they could be used to hide its knives!"

The Hunter was at a loss, I fear, and in his loyalty to his fellow hunters, farmers and other settlers, and to Rhodes himself, could not understand my grief.

I was eventually able to bring myself under control, and gratefully accepted the cloth he offered to dry my eyes. And there in that smoke and in the poor shade of the little tents I seized his hands and made what confession I could.

"I am sorry, dear man," I said. "But I am not any longer the girl who taught you to sin for her own pleasure. I warned you then that I was not to be loved, but only enjoyed, but even I could not have foreseen how the stain of this undertaking would mark me. You are not at fault, please believe me, it is only my naiveté, a strange weakness for such as me to confess to, that wounds me so.

"Perhaps a hard earned maturity was among the gifts that Miss Terry hoped I'd gain through this experience. I suppose it may in time prove valuable to me, but like gold with nowhere to spend it, at the moment I can only feel its weight.

"Take me to that train, and when I am gone forget this Paulette and remember only she who brought you joy. Find the wife you need, whether here or in England if you must, and never tell her of me. Let her be innocent and believe that the things you do to please her are among the mysteries of the Order of Men. You will do so, you will be happy with her as you never could have been with me."

And there I kissed him, and his lips did not part, and he treated me with every courtesy until I was safely aboard that Plumtree train.

It was not until I was well away that I discovered his parting gift; a page torn from a favorite book of Mr. Kipling's smaller writings. I affix it here, a fitting epitaph for a love I had encouraged only to let die, and for the girl that I'd lost in Africa.

A fool there was and he made his prayer
(Even as you or I!)
To a rag and a bone and a hank of hair,
(We called her the woman who did not care),
But the fool he called her his lady fair--
(Even as you or I!)

Oh, the years we waste and the tears we waste,
And the work of our head and hand
Belong to the woman who did not know
(And now we know that she never could know)
And did not understand!

A fool there was and his goods he spent,
(Even as you or I!)
Honour and faith and a sure intent
(And it wasn't the least what the lady meant),
But a fool must follow his natural bent
(Even as you or I!)

Oh, the toil we lost and the spoil we lost
And the excellent things we planned
Belong to the woman who didn't know why
(And now we know that she never knew why)
And did not understand!

The fool was stripped to his foolish hide,
(Even as you or I!)
Which she might have seen when she threw him aside--
(But it isn't on record the lady tried)

Royal Blood

So some of him lived but the most of him died--
(Even as you or I!)

``And it isn't the shame and it isn't the blame
That stings like a white-hot brand--
It's coming to know that she never knew why
(Seeing, at last, she could never know why)
And never could understand!''

Chapter 36

Comings and goings—An eternal's petulance—Note sent 'round to Holmes—An unusual reply—The Diogenes Club —Not the expected gathering—A tragedy revealed— Lady Ellen's lesson continued—Rich beyond my wildest dreams—A girl went to Africa, a woman looks to America.

My return trip approximated the route I had taken when coming to Africa, but where the first was, despite occasional doldrums, and adventure, the latter seemed merely a chore. Trains and airships and steamers were tied together, roughly lassoed in the noose of what remained of the generous travel allowance Rhodes has provided me. Where there was opportunity (and even at times when such windows were precariously brief) I fed to repletion, recklessly and angrily, and brutally.

There will no doubt be tales sparked by *this* passage of Paulette Monot told in my ports of call for generations to come. In short I was like a young girl in the throes of her first menses, indulging in a frightened tantrum at bidding farewell to her girlhood and not yet willing to Though I had no shortage of clothes fit for travel, and ample opportunities to purchase more, I stubbornly stayed within the outfits that had served me in the Bush, only washing these poor faded and tattered things when the need became dire. In my personal toilet I was more recalcitrant still; my hair remained a yellow thicket where it escaped from the hats that were my constant companions when in public, and I abstained from the ablutions and powders that society expects its women to endure. In short I likely appeared a mad creature to those fated to travel in my company, and if that proved an impediment to socializing I was all the more happy for it. Money, I soon discovered, is the most potent of all human cosmetics, and I spent the former lavishly in order to avoid subjecting myself to the latter.

It was not until I finally arrived in London, and found my former rooms unchanged (and unaired!), that I succumbed again to the demands of appearance. I knew that until my stay in that city was concluded, the mission that I had undertaken, and that had cost me so dearly, would not be truly finished, nor would I be rewarded. Perhaps I also craved the congratulations of the Lady of the City, and hoped that such a maternal pat on the head for a job well done would provide a balm that would heal that for which I had yet to find remedy.

So once the rooms were again made comfortable, I bathed, and powdered, and perfumed, and selecting the best of my outfits (which were now a season old, and would not do for exalted company), took myself out into the streets and spent much of the rest of my advance on the sort of finery whose moment in the mode is as brief as the life of a mayfly. Thus armed, I returned to my apartment and sent a message 'round to Baker Street by courier, announcing my return and my desire for a meeting as soon as such could be arranged. Since my initial recruitment had been at the hands of Mr. Holmes, it seemed appropriate that I should schedule my report through him as well.

For several days I received no reply, but though the waiting chafed me, I was not so bold as to go unbidden to the

Great Detective's address, and even less inclined to importune upon the Lady of the City. So I found what amusement I could in the plays of the season and, in my newfound recklessness, even indulged in a bit of hunting among the streets and alleyways where I had once refrained from predation in recognition of my status as a guest in that ancient and oft celebrated town.

When a response to my message did arrive, it was not as I'd anticipated. The sheet of notepaper upon which is was penned bore the imprint of the Diogenes Club, an establishment of which I had never heard, and the hand itself was unfamiliar to me, though I had had occasion enough to become familiar with the Great Detective's distinctive handwriting while my adventure had been in the planning stages.

"My dear Miss Monot," it read, "we are grateful for your safe return and all agog over the success of your undertaking. Please be prepared to meet the principals involved for lunch tomorrow at the Diogenes Club," and here it included an address near Carlton Street, which I have been asked not to publish.

"You will be welcomed into the Stranger's Room, which is reserved for guests, upon your arrival. Please do not stray into any of the adjoining chambers, as members of the public are not welcome there and a disturbance would unnecessarily delay our proceedings." The signature affixed, which was no more familiar to me than the script itself, read simply, "

Holmes was not a little nonplussed by this message, knowing well that my associates were possessed of powerful enemies who might seek advantage by just this sort of subterfuge; but I determined to comply with its request nonetheless, if only to solve the mysteries thus presented to me. I did of course take the precaution of freshly charging and pocketing my pepper-box, believing that it were better to endure the Detective's amusement at my being so armed than to find myself without it when in need.

Thus as the appointed hour approached I bedecked myself in my new finery to full effect, and arranged for a Hansom cab. (My Coilcycle of course, having sustained great damage in Africa, was following a slower path home than the one which I had travelled; and in truth I had begun to believe that such transport was a bit on the rough-and-ready side for a woman of my accomplishments, and planned to sell it off in order to purchase a steam carriage upon my return to America.) The address proved to belong to a nondescript doorway, and I lingered there for a moment in indecision until a rather corpulent individual approached and, after confirming my name, proceeded to lead me through an inner hallway and into a nicely appointed club room.

There I immediately perceived Lady Ellen and Mr. Rhodes, as well as a gentleman unknown to me who stood as I entered, his distinguished visage showing the clear signs of recent and enduring grief. My escort then closed the door behind us and waved me to a seat.

"Miss Monot," he began, "I believe you are acquainted with Ellen Terry and Mr. Rhodes, and allow me to introduce you to Dr. John Watson, whose chronicles of Sherlock Holmes' adventures you might be familiar with." I curtsied to the gentleman indicated, and assembled myself in the seat provided.

"But where is Holmes?" I asked.

"I am Holmes," the heavy-set gentleman replied, "Or rather Mycroft Holmes, the brother of the Consulting Detective I believe you expected to find here."

"Sherlock Holmes is gone!" the man introduced to me as Dr. Watson suddenly cried out, his composure failing him, "A victim of the beast Professor Moriarty, who proved to be his match at last." This of course shocked me, and I turned to Miss Terry, blurting, "But surely there is something we can do?"

The Mistress of the City raised her gloved hand to stop me, and fixed me with her inimitable eyes, which froze me in place despite the tinted glasses which had become a constant accessory to my wardrobe.

"Pray consider the lessons you've so recently learned, my dear Paulette," she said. "There are occasions when the interest of our people run with those of Mr. Holmes, and others when Professor Moriarty's ambitions better mirror our own. We are not, after all, a force for the public benefit; it is our own needs we must always look to. Those who deal with us know we cannot be assumed to align ourselves with any particular cause." And here she cast an almost flirtatious glance at Rhodes, who harrumphed irritably.

"I would that Sherlock had never turned to such monsters!" Watson replied, slapping his hand on his desk in fury.Here Mycroft interjected, and as he spoke I found I could almost see the Great Detective's ascetic profile peering out of the suet pudding of his face.

"Hush, John," he said. "You know as well as I that without the aid of Ellen Terry my brother's resume would be far less impressive than it is. Her people are a force of nature, and Sherlock knew, as do you, that sometimes the rain will wash away a track, but that same downpour might soften the ground elsewhere to allow a spoor to be taken. We must neither curse nor bless the ways of the weather or the kin, but only work with them as we can."

"Ahem!" said Rhodes, who had watched the preceding with an ill-concealed impatience. "A tragedy no doubt. A great loss to England. I share in your grief. But this is not a time for philosophy, but for business!" He intoned the latter in a breathy manner more often reserved for prayer.

Miss Terry stood at this, and placed a dainty hand on my shoulder.

"Please continue, Cecil, I know your impatience when it comes to divesting yourself of money."

The man tut-tutted and mumbled prissily, but pulled a tablet to himself and an ink pen, and fixed me with a weighing eye.

"You have fulfilled your pledge in every detail, Miss Monot. In fact, you might be surprised to know that we have had word just this morning that the African Despot who so impeded the destined fate of Matabeleland has shed his earthly coil!"

I could not hold back a gasp, but Ellen gripped my shoulder painfully, and I restrained myself from any further outburst.

"Yes, quite," said Rhodes. "And I believe I am prepared to berather generous with your recompense." He reached into a portmanteau at his side and pulled out a brick of bank notes. "First, to assist in your travel back to your native land, I've arranged for a cash payment that I trust you will find quite adequate." He pushed the currency toward me and I accepted it without counting, noting that Miss Terry's eyes were still on the magnate.

"And then," he continued, putting pen to paper "I am prepared to transfer funds in this amount to whatever account you wish, to assure your future comfort." He scribbled a figure that quite took my breath away, but before I could respond Ellen took the pen from his hand, crossed out the numerals he had written, and scratched out a number larger still.

"This is quite generous of you, Cecil," she purred. "I believe Miss Monot accepts."

Rhodes looked as if he thought to argue, but meeting those bewitching grey eyes appeared to take the fight clean out of him.

"Yes, yes it is," he mumbled.

With that business concluded Miss Terry bade me provide him with the appropriate information concerning my banking institution and then, with the most delicate urging of her hand, drew me to my feet.

"Our enterprise is thus brought to a close, gentlemen," she said. "Cecil dear, it is always a pleasure. Dr. Watson and Mycroft, we must meet again very soon; for I do believe there is every possibility that we can find a point in this matter where our interests converge."

And then she led me out into the street, and into a life of riches I could never before have imagined.

She kissed my cheek in parting, and the weight of Rhodes' bills in my pocket, and the exorbitant Letter of Credit, seemed to somewhat balance the burden that I had carried in my heart from Africa. I would invest the latter, of course, and in doing so assure that there would be riches enough to allow my line to flourish long into the future.

And what better, and more bitter, thing to invest in than the limitless promise of a new country? Of Rhodesia?

It would, after all, be the civilized thing to do.

FINIS

About the Author

Bruce Woods

Bruce Woods is a professional writer/editor with more than 30 years in magazine publishing, having worked as editor of *Mother Earth News* and *Alaska Magazine*, among others, and has published both nonfiction and poetry books. *Prairie Schooner* magazine featured his work in its "Writing from Alaska" issue. His *Birdhouse Book*, brought out by Sterling/Lark, is still in print and has sold more than 100,000 copies.

After leaving the editor's position at *Alaska Magazine* in late 1998, Woods began a second career in External Affairs for the Alaska Region of the U.S. Fish and Wildlife Service. Eventually serving as the de facto writer/editor for the agency's largest region, as well as providing information and an initial contact point for state, national, and international media on topics affecting Alaska's often controversial wildlife and land management issues, Woods retired in the spring of 2013 in order to focus on fiction writing.

His *Hearts of Darkness* trilogy, the first two volumes of which, *Royal Blood* and *Dragon Blood,* are scheduled for publication by Penmore Press in 2019.

In addition to the *Birdhouse Book* referenced above, Woods has published three nonfiction volumes and several books of poetry with small presses. During his magazine editing career he also served as editor/contributor to numerous nonfiction volumes. Several of his essays have been anthologized, as well.

Woods currently lives in Anchorage, Alaska with his wife Mary and his two cats, Lucy Fur and Boswell. Gardening and bicycling (the latter usually upon a single-speed road bike named "Yellow Snow" that he built from an old track frame bought online) are chief among his many interests outside of reading and writing. He has two children, Ethan, who studied music composition at Bennington College and now resides in Asheville, N.C., and his daughter Alice, who recently graduated from Minneapolis College of Art and Design and currently lives in Minneapolis.

If You Enjoyed This Book
Visit

PENMORE PRESS

www.penmorepress.com

Rembrandt's
Angel
by
Steven Moore

A Neo-Nazi conspiracy threatens Europe...

Esther Brookstone's life is at a crossroads. A Scotland Yard inspector who specializes in stolen art, she's reluctantly considering retirement. A three-time widow, she can't quite decide whether paramour and colleague Interpol Agent Bastiann van Coevorden should be husband number four. Decisions are put on hold while she and Bastiann set out to thwart a neo-Nazi conspiracy financed in part by artworks stolen during World War II. Among the stolen art is the masterpiece "An Angel with Titus' Features," a work Esther obsesses about recovering.

The case sends the intrepid pair on an international hunt spanning several European countries and the Amazon jungle. Evading capture and thwarting death, Esther and Bastiann prove time and again that adrenaline-spiked adventures aren't just for the young.

PENMORE PRESS
www.penmorepress.com

A Gathering of Vultures

Donald Michael Platt

Murder, mutilation, and carrion.... in paradise?

"There shall the vultures also be gathered, every one with her mate." - ISAIAH 34:15

Professional ballroom dancers Terri and Rick Hamilton aspire to be world champions. Unfortunately, Terri's recurring back and health problems place that goal well out of reach. They travel to Terri's birthplace, Florianópolis, on the scenic island of Santa Catarina off the coast of Brazil to vacation and visit their best friends and mentors.

Along the picturesque beaches, dead penguins and eviscerated bodies wash up on the shores of paradise, and Antarctic blasts play counterpoint to the tropical storms that rock the island. The scenic wonder is home not only to urubús, a unique sub-species of the black vulture, but also to a clique of mysterious women who offer Terri perfect health and the promise of fame—at a terrible price.

PENMORE PRESS
www.penmorepress.com

Midshipman Graham and the
Battle of
Abukir

by

James Boschert

It is midsummer of 1799 and the British Navy in the Mediterranean Theater of operations. Napoleon has brought the best soldiers and scientists from France to claim Egypt and replace the Turkish empire with one of his own making, but the debacle at Acre has caused the brilliant general to retreat to Cairo.

Commodore Sir Sidney Smith and the Turkish army land at the strategically critical fortress of Abukir, on the northern coast of Egypt. Here Smith plans to further the reversal of Napoleon's fortunes. Unfortunately, the Turks badly underestimate the speed, strength, and resolve of the French Army, and the ensuing battle becomes one of the worst defeats in Arab history.

Young Midshipman Duncan Graham is anxious to get ahead in the British Navy, but has many hurdles to overcome. Without any familial privileges to smooth his way, he can only advance through merit. The fires of war prove his mettle, but during an expedition to obtain desperately needed fresh water – and an illegal duel – a French patrol drives off the boats, and Graham is left stranded on shore. It now becomes a question of evasion and survival with the help of a British spy. Graham has to become very adaptable in order to avoid detection by the French police, and he must help the spy facilitate a daring escape by sea in order to get back to the British squadron.

*"Midshipman Graham and The Battle of Abukir i*s both a rousing Napoleonic naval yarn and a convincing coming of age story. The battle scenes are riveting and powerful, the exotic Egyptian locales colorfully rendered."* – John Danielski, author of *Capital's Punishment*

PENMORE PRESS
www.penmorepress.com

A Turning Wind

by

J. G Harlond

LUDO DA PORTOVENERE, ONE TIME CORSAIR, SOMETIME MERCHANT, SECRET AGENT OF MONARCHS, SERVANT OF NONE.

From the trading colony of Goa to the royal courts of England and Spain, Ludo da Portovenere completes difficult and dangerous secret commissions on his own terms and for his own reasons. But, as these tasks bring him closer to success, Ludo is forced to confront dangerous secrets of his own. While Ludo pursues a delicate mission for the English queen in the Spanish royal court, Alina, Baroness Metherall, faces challenges and dangers of her own as she tries to come to terms with what it means to be married to one person and love another. Ultimately, Ludo and Alina must decide who they really are, and to what extent their shared past should influence their future.

"Harlond's brilliantly realized portrait of the sea-trade in 17th century is a gem...Ludo is a great character with wit, intelligence and daring. Exploiting his position as an envoy between Charles I and the Spanish court results in a seafaring novel of danger and double-dealing. Highly recommended." Deborah Swift, author of Pleasing Mr Pepys

"Ms. Harlond details a credible, intricate world of deals and alliances, threats and opportunities, uncertainty and trust, in which her hero, the wily Genoese merchant Ludo da Portovenere, must tread with extreme caution. Let's hear yet more of him!" --Antoine Vanner, author of The Dawlish Chronicles series.

penmorepress.com